There was only need.

The same need that had found her in his bed, beneath him, begging for every filthy thing he'd done for her, to her. Regina melted against him, hanging on to every sliver of emotion she saw play across his face.

Beneath the obvious anger there was that same need she felt burning through her system. The flush running just beneath his skin was the same as the night he'd taken her to unimaginable heights in his bed. Yes, she was here for another round of that, even if it was because he was so furious with her that devouring her was the only way he could temper his anger.

Too needy to be patient, she licked her dry lips and opened her mouth to speak.

"What can I do, Aléx?"

His lips turned up in the corners, giving his classically handsome features a sinister twist.

"You can start by making up for the little charade you played on me by marrying me and giving me the child you owe me."

Well damn. Of all the things she'd expected, no, wanted to hear from him, it sure as hell wasn't that.

A dazzling new duet for Harlequin Presents from author LaQuette.

Crowning a Devereaux

By royal decree, the Devereaux sisters will be crowned!

Identical twins and business partners Reigna and Regina Devereaux were born to lead—they just didn't realize that included a kingdom.

When ex-lover Jasiri charges back into Reigna's life with an arranged-marriage offer, she never imagined it would mean becoming his crown princess! But he's offering to return to her the inheritance that he was wrongfully given... So Reigna says "I do"...only to find that even royal duty cannot keep their attraction from roaring back to life!

Royal Bride Demand

When Regina takes her twin sister's place at a royal function on Obsidian Island, she never imagined she'd end up falling into bed with Aléxandros—the king! With their chemistry undeniable and the monarchy without an heir, he has a proposition for her—marry him and bear his child! But can Regina resist falling for the enigmatic ruler...?

The King's Pregnancy Proposition

Both available now!

THE KING'S PREGNANCY PROPOSITION

LaQUETTE

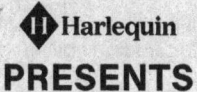

PRESENTS

If you purchased this book without a cover you should be aware that this book is stolen property. It was reported as "unsold and destroyed" to the publisher, and neither the author nor the publisher has received any payment for this "stripped book."

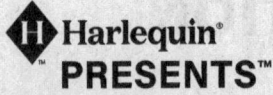

Harlequin® PRESENTS™

Recycling programs for this product may not exist in your area.

ISBN-13: 978-1-335-21936-7

The King's Pregnancy Proposition

Copyright © 2025 by Laquette R. Holmes

All rights reserved. No part of this book may be used or reproduced in any manner whatsoever without written permission.

Without limiting the author's and publisher's exclusive rights, any unauthorized use of this publication to train generative artificial intelligence (AI) technologies is expressly prohibited.

This is a work of fiction. Names, characters, places and incidents are either the product of the author's imagination or are used fictitiously. Any resemblance to actual persons, living or dead, businesses, companies, events or locales is entirely coincidental.

For questions and comments about the quality of this book, please contact us at CustomerService@Harlequin.com.

TM and ® are trademarks of Harlequin Enterprises ULC.

Harlequin Enterprises ULC
22 Adelaide St. West, 41st Floor
Toronto, Ontario M5H 4E3, Canada
www.Harlequin.com

HarperCollins Publishers
Macken House, 39/40 Mayor Street Upper,
Dublin 1, D01 C9W8, Ireland
www.HarperCollins.com

Printed in U.S.A.

A 2021 Vivian Award finalist and DEIA activist in the romance industry, **LaQuette** writes sexy, stylish and sensational romance. She crafts dramatic, emotionally epic tales that are deeply pigmented by reality's paintbrush. This Brooklyn native writes unapologetically bold, character-driven stories. Her novels feature diverse ensemble casts who are confident in their right to appear on the page. Contact: dot.cards/laquette

Books by LaQuette

Harlequin Presents

Crowning a Devereaux
Royal Bride Demand

Harlequin Desire

Devereaux Inc.
A Very Intimate Takeover
Backstage Benefits
One Night Expectations
Secret Heir for Christmas

Visit the Author Profile page
at Harlequin.com for more titles.

To my sister, Ebony. We may not be twins,
but it's reassuring to know there's someone
in the world who don't play about me.

CHAPTER ONE

"ALÉX, I'M NOT quite sure what you hope to gain by dragging this out. You're a king. You have a responsibility to marry and produce an heir. We both know I'm the best choice for a consort. I've always been the best choice for a consort. Why are you dragging your feet?"

King Aléxandros of Obsidian Island internally cringed as he listened to the words coming out of Lady Katia's mouth. It wasn't as though Aléx hadn't heard these things from his late parents and his royal advisors seemingly since birth. He'd been reared in the expectation that he would fulfill this particular duty since he drew his first breath.

Aléx had also been taught the skill of keeping one's feelings from public view. Yet when Lady Katia slid an unwanted hand on his thigh, his outrage at being touched so intimately without his permission seeped out through the taut muscles of his face. His quick hand pried her claws from his person and placed them atop the elaborate gold-and-black marble bar they were seated at.

"Lady Katia, you forget your place. As a member of the Obsidian Court, the privilege of speaking to me with such familiarity hasn't been given to you. Please address me as is proper, King Aléxandros, Your Majesty, or Sire."

Aléx watched as Lady Katia's thin, classic features pulled tightly into sharp lines at his reprisal. She was part of the Obsidian aristocracy. A woman who had been bred to believe she and her ilk were better than people who didn't have aristocratic blood in their veins. The only people who were better were royals, which was why she'd been campaigning through various methods to situate herself as the perfect consort for the unmarried king. She and every other single woman at court made no secret of their desire to be his queen. As a result, Aléx never dated or slept with anyone at court, not since the first and only time ended so horribly.

Not since he'd lost everything.

Never again.

Lesson learned, Aléx was extremely selective of the women he chose to bed. They could have nothing to do with royal or aristocratic life, and most importantly, they couldn't expect more than physical release.

Yes, he had a duty to marry and procreate,

and he would eventually fulfill that duty. But until he was sure he'd found someone he could trust, someone who would stand by him and choose him and the family they created over everything and everyone else, including the crown, he would remain single. His past demanded that he accept nothing less. And since Katia's only goal was the clout and wealth associated with being the king's consort, there was no way in hell he'd ever choose her as his wife.

He knew she'd never want to hear that. This standoff they were currently engaged in was proof of that. Being turned away so blatantly wouldn't sit well with a woman like her. The stiff shoulders and pointed stare she leveled at him after his reprisal confirmed every instinct he had about Katia. At all costs, he needed to keep her away from him.

"Your Majesty?"

A sultry voice that he barely recognized filled his senses, pulling his gaze from the cold ice of Katia's blue gaze to a rich warmth the color of dark cognac drawing him in.

"I'm sorry to interrupt, but you told me to find you here for our meeting. Are you still available?"

Aléx took in the beauty before him. Reigna Devereaux, the CEO of Gemini Queens Cosmetics. She was a regular attendee at Obsidian

Island's annual Commerce Gala. But never in all their interactions had she ever caught his notice so completely.

Her dark hair was braided into an intricate pattern that spoke to her heritage as an African American woman, putting her cultural pride on display for all to see. Her lips were covered in a matte red lipstick that artfully highlighted a mouth that made him wonder how it compared to the sweet berries that grew in the wild forested soil of his land.

He stood to his full height of six feet two inches, noticing that even in her impossibly high heels, she barely reached the middle of his chest. Tiny though she might have been, there was confidence in the way she stood in those slinky, strappy heels and the one-shouldered bodycon red cocktail dress that caressed her ample, plus-sized curves.

That self-assurance called to him, and he had to fight his natural urge to get closer to her, to lean into her and take in every glorious inch she possessed.

"Absolutely," he replied, noting the spark of mischief that flashed in the woman's eyes. "I've been looking forward to speaking to you all evening."

With his eyes still locked on to Reigna's, Aléx

said, "Please excuse me, Lady Katia. I must attend to a most urgent matter."

Before Katia could reply, he extended his arm to Reigna, waiting for her to wrap her hand around his bicep. When she did, his body tensed, but not in revulsion as it had with Katia. This was excitement mixed with a healthy dose of satisfaction of knowing what her touch felt like, even through the fine threads of his tailor-made tuxedo jacket.

"Shall we, Ms. Devereaux?"

He lifted a brow, waiting for her response, delighting at the devious curl of her lips and the devilish grin that resulted.

"Certainly, Your Majesty."

Katia completely forgotten, Aléx moved away from the bar and through the grand ballroom of the largest luxury hotel in his country.

"Would you mind following me to my suite? I'm afraid if we remain in any of the public areas of the hotel, all eyes will remain on us. I promise you will be perfectly safe."

She conceded with a nod to Aléx as two large men converged and fell in step at a comfortable distance behind them. She smiled up at him with that same mischievous grin.

"Oh, dear King Aléxandros, I know I'll be perfectly safe in your suite. You know just as well as I that starting an international incident with a Devereaux wouldn't be good for you or your country."

He couldn't help the genuine chuckle that rumbled in his chest and out of his throat. There was that poise he'd seen in her stance when she'd interrupted his tense exchange with Katia. Up close, with no distractions between them, it was even more brilliant than before.

His guards were positioned all throughout the building, so Aléx had no fear of her apparent bodyguards pulling up their rear.

He directed her toward the private elevator to the penthouse and noticed that two other men joined two of his own at the doors.

"It appears your security team is just as thorough as mine. I wouldn't be surprised if your men are already in place when we exit the elevator as well."

"Of course they are," she replied. "You don't get to be a woman as successful as me by not taking your safety seriously, even in the presence of kings."

The elevator reached the penthouse floor. The doors opened following a soft ding, and just as he'd surmised, in the corridor there were extra security members he assumed were part of her team, standing side by side with his own.

He didn't know how she'd managed to get

clearance to do this, but there was something enticing about the fact that she wielded enough command to thwart a king if she chose to.

Possessing so much power himself meant Aléx always had to be mindful of the positions he put people in, making sure he wasn't taking advantage of the immediate dynamic that came when you were the ruler of a nation dealing with a common person.

Reigna stepped into his suite and sat in an armchair in the living room before he'd even offered her a seat, crossing one thick, enticing leg over the other while offering him a captivating smile. It was a power move; he was certain of that. Reigna Devereaux didn't ask for permission. She simply did what she wanted because she was always in control.

Reigna Devereaux was not a common person. How he'd missed that fact in all their polite exchanges over the years, he didn't know. But tonight, more than anything or anyone else, Aléx understood that this woman was both temptation and a threat tied together in a sexy bow.

"Considering we've said less than a handful of words to one another over the years, how did you know I would welcome your little ruse to get me away from Lady Katia, Ms. Devereaux?"

Regina Devereaux relaxed a little in her

chair. Hearing him use her surname meant she wouldn't have to keep reminding herself to answer when he called her by her twin sister's name, Reigna.

She'd agreed to represent Gemini Queens by pretending to be Reigna at this fancy gala while the real Reigna was playing the part of the dutiful new queen of Nyeusi. Yes, Reigna and her husband, Jasiri, were the newly installed king and queen of Nyeusi. Jasiri's ascension to the throne was an unexpected event devised to save the kingdom from his power-hungry uncle. With the Nyeusian monarchy so unstable, Reigna had begged Regina not just to take her place, but to pretend to be her at this gala.

According to Reigna, Aléxandros was a staunch stick-in-the-mud who demanded the heads of the top-selling foreign companies in his country meet once a year at this gala. It was essentially a way for the king to put faces to the people Obsidian Island did business with. It seemed a bit micromanage-y for Regina's tastes. However, with as much revenue as Gemini Queens garnered from this particular business relationship, Regina had given in to her sister and agreed to cosplay as Reigna the way no other person in the world could.

Her sister was the one who loved the limelight and exuded confidence in social settings. Regina was self-possessed, but usually in numbers and scientific formulas and equations. Dealing with people was an altogether different matter. But when she'd seen that woman pushing herself uninvited into the king's space, something protective in her flashed hot, forcing Regina into action.

"I'm a woman in corporate America; I can spot uninvited and inappropriate attention and action a mile away. Even with your cool facade, you seemed tense. That was especially true when your speaking companion touched you. I figured I'd do for you what's been done for me dozens of times when I found myself in similar situations, where cursing fools out or smacking fire out of them would cause me and my business more harm than good."

The king mouthed *smacking fire out of them* as if he were testing the weight and meaning of the phrase, and Regina couldn't help but chuckle. This man was a king. He'd probably never encountered such language, figurative or otherwise, in his rarified circles.

Regina gave herself a mental shake at the word *rarified*. She was part of a billionaire family; she too moved in rarified circles. But the Devereauxs had kept their feet, and their sensibilities, firmly planted in Brooklyn, meaning it wasn't every day they were seated in the private company of actual royalty.

Reigna was going to owe her big-time for this particular game of twin swap.

Not only was being the face of Gemini Queens far outside her skill set, but this king with his thick midnight-black hair and Caribbean-blue eyes was seriously messing with her John Stamos fixation.

For anyone who hadn't noticed, John Stamos was fine long before he was Uncle Jesse on *Full House*. Although it was before her time, she'd found a couple of clips of him on *General Hospital* playing the character Blackie Parrish on YouTube. Yes, he was fine even back then too.

King Aléxandros was, for lack of a better word, HAWT!

Yes, HAWT.

His level of sexy, with his rippled muscles peeking through the expertly crafted tuxedo, coupled with that distinguished yet powerful gentleman affect he was giving off, could not be contained or explained in the simple three-lettered spelling of the word. It needed an extra letter, an alternate spelling, and exaggerated pronunciation just to scratch the surface of how attractive and enigmatic this man was. Attractive enough that while she'd faithfully worshipped at John Stamos's altar of fine, the king was making her seriously think of switching her allegiance from the Hollywood heartthrob to this revered monarch.

"Ms. Devereaux." The king's rich voice broke through her thoughts, bringing her attention directly to his face. His jaw was strong and clean-shaven, and along with his overall countenance, just exuded authority. "As a king, people scurry to attend to my commands or what they think I want. Very few people look beyond the crown to consider what I might need."

The lines around his face softened as he unbuttoned his jacket and sat on the ottoman directly in front of her. The cool scent of his cologne tickled her senses, forcing her to fight the powerful urge to shove her nose in his neck and fill her lungs to their capacity with the smell of him.

"Thank you for looking beyond the crown and seeing the man in need."

He was sharing his vulnerability with her, and that fact made desire twist a knot in her gut. A man who held might at his fingertips but still managed to understand and express his own vulnerability? She was sure it had to be stronger than any controlled substance on the planet.

She'd never been tempted once in her life to indulge in substance abuse. But everything she'd seen from this man tonight, especially now when he was laying his guard down, it made her want to crawl into his lap and wrap her arms around those broad shoulders she was certain were holding the weight of the world.

"I know what it's like for people to not see you, to never allow you to be your authentic and individual self. I'm just glad I happened to see what was going on. No one should be touched without their consent. You being a king or a man shouldn't mean you're excluded from that expectation."

A flash of fire in his eyes called to the twin flame burning in her gut. After she'd just told this man no one should touch him without his consent, all she wanted to do was touch him—hell, taste him, if he'd allow it.

God, why must I have home training and be so principled? Why can't I be like that thirsty heifer downstairs and just take what I want?

She closed her eyes and answered her own question.

Because you're not gross, Regina. You actually care about other human beings.

That fact hadn't meant she'd always been treated with the same care and respect she gave to others. She didn't play games, at least not usually, and that seemed to be a major turnoff to the men that crossed her path. If she was interested in something long-term, she didn't try to trick men into being with her. When you grew up living in someone else's shadow, appearing invisible to others was a fate worse than death. So she made a habit of saying exactly what she meant. At least then, potential suitors would jump ship early, and she wouldn't have to go through the heartache and hurt of falling for someone who didn't want what she wanted and didn't see the value in her.

"Ms. Devereaux."

The king's voice pulled her out of her head and made her focus on him. That same fire was still there burning between them, no matter how she fought to douse it.

"Please know that you can absolutely reply no to this question, and there will be no reprisals for your company and the business you do on Obsidian Island."

Intrigued, she nodded, wondering what the king would say next.

"Would you be amenable to me kissing you?"

The woman with home training should've said no. The accomplished businesswoman and scientist should've said no. But when she opened her mouth, the only thing that toppled out was, "Hell yes."

A satisfied smile curled his lips as he reached for her, pulling her into his lap and locking his mouth to hers.

She went willingly, and matched his enthusiasm, opening for him with the slightest pressure of his tongue against her bottom lip.

His fingers threaded into her braids, making the sensitive flesh there tingle. Her resulting moan was rewarded with his hand tightening on her thigh, holding her securely against him.

He was a king, a man who was polished and refined to shine like new money. But he kissed like a street brawler. His movements fierce, lacking the poised control and elegance his station in life demanded. He was consuming her with that kiss, and simultaneously remaking her one cell at a time. She would be forever changed after this, and judging from the way her nipples hardened and her sex throbbed, she was perfectly okay with that as long as he kept doing what he was doing.

God, please let him keep doing what he's doing.

As if he'd heard her thoughts, Aléxandros tore his mouth away from hers, leaving them both panting. There was a slightly feral look in his gaze that did nothing to quench the heat and the need for this man building inside her.

He opened his mouth to speak, but she preempted him, holding up her hands.

"Just in case you want to ask me if it's okay to invade my personal space even further, and God willing, in much more detail, just know I am one hundred percent amenable to whatever you have in mind."

He closed his eyes as he pulled her closer to him, the hard swell of his flesh pressing against her thigh and letting her see for herself she wasn't the only one affected by their unexpected chemistry.

He pressed his forehead to hers and groaned as if he ached for something, anything to satisfy whatever this was building between them.

"From the moment you captured my notice, I knew two things, Ms. Devereaux."

She pulled away, locking into his gaze as he continued to speak.

"One, you are the most alluring woman I've ever seen, and two, you're dangerous."

CHAPTER TWO

SHE GATHERED WHAT little of her senses remained and whispered, "Does that mean you'd like me to leave?"

He shoved his hand under her knees and his other arm around her waist just before he stood with her cradled against him like she was a real-life Disney princess.

"The only place I want you is in my bed. If you don't want that too, I need to know now."

She circled her arms around his neck, pressing her breasts into the hard wall of him.

"One hundred percent amenable. Isn't that what I said?"

She hadn't been kidding when she'd said it. She was ready for anything and everything this king wanted to do to her.

If she were thinking with her brain, she'd acknowledge how bad an idea sleeping with this man was. He was a whole king, a man with unbelievable power who, if he chose to, could use that power to make her life a living hell. Not to mention, one-night stands with men connected in tangible ways to her business made this uncharacteristic "to hell with it" attitude she was currently sporting problematic and unwise. That rational thought was trying to gain some traction by tugging at the back of her mind. But then he looked at her, and rational thought left the building with no plans on returning anytime soon.

His eyes narrowed, intensifying the fire burning in them. She thought he was going to speak again, possibly be the one to exercise some good sense in this situation, because she certainly wasn't capable of that in this moment. Instead, he took long steps out of the room, walking through an opened door that led to one of the largest hotel bedrooms she'd ever seen. This suite really was made for a king.

He kicked the door closed, and the next thing she knew, she was standing—well, barely standing, considering how her legs felt like limp noodles suddenly—on the prettiest pair of strappy platform heels she owned.

He yanked off his tie and jacket and began undoing the diamond cuff links at his wrist. She thought he'd walk away and put them in a secure place. She was wrong. He pulled them off and discarded them on the foot bench like they were knockoffs being sold by a street vendor in Brooklyn.

His shirt was gone next, and when his smooth, tanned skin came into view, without thought she stepped closer to him, touching his skin reverently.

"It really should be illegal for you to be this fine and feel this good at the same time."

"Flattery will get you everything you want, Ms. Devereaux. But first, I need a bit of what I want."

His large hands covered her shoulders and turned her away from him.

Slowly, painfully so, his fingers found her zipper. He was so exacting and punishing with his slowness, she was convinced she could feel every tooth of her zipper release until it reached its end in the middle of her back.

As deliberate as he was with unzipping her dress, he was as driven to shove it down her body and expose her to him.

The hunger in his gaze was palpable. She could feel it sweep across her sensitive flesh as if he'd reached out and touched her. He was damn near salivating, which was another plus in the tally she was keeping on him. He was powerful, yet not afraid to show vulnerability, and by the way he was sizing her up and walking her backward to his bed, he liked thick girls too.

Okay, Mr. King!

Regina and her twin had always been plus-sized. A fact they were both fine with. They loved their bodies and killed it at the fashion game, proving repeatedly that fluffy was indeed fabulous.

Just because Regina loved her body and knew she was everything a man could want or desire, it didn't mean she hadn't run into men who didn't see her value. She didn't waste time, effort, or thought on those men.

If the king had shown anything but uncontrollable desire when he'd taken off her clothes, she would've walked out of this room in her bra, panties and heels while telling him to kiss her round ass as she left.

Fortunately for them both, Aléxandros seemed enthralled and utterly captivated by her curves.

As soon as she was spread out against the expensive linens, Aléxandros lost whatever restraint he had. He was out of his pants and silk boxers in what seemed like an instant, proudly displaying the length and girth of what by anyone's standards was an impressive erection.

She leaned up to grab for it, and he pushed her greedy hand away.

"Soon, but not yet. You can't present such a fine selection to a man and not expect him to feast."

That was the only warning she had before he kissed his way down her body, stopping to pull the cups of her strapless bra down to take one and then the other pert nipple in his mouth.

He hovered over her soft stomach, allowing his hands and lips to worship her there too. And then he finally, with the deliberate patience of a man intending to savor his meal, removed her lace panties, taking a moment to inhale her essence as if it was the most wonderful thing he'd ever encountered.

The first stroke of his fingers against the delicate flesh of her mound made her tremble to her core. Why was the feel of him against her flesh so familiar, as if her body had prior experience with this king?

He opened her to him, gathering her waiting arousal and spreading it over the tender flesh with his gentle touch. Pleasure uncoiled at her core, drawing a needy moan from her.

"Yes," he moaned in reply as he slipped one and then two digits inside her. "I want to hear you moan pretty for me. Just like that."

His words drew another deep moan from her, and she had to wonder how he could sound so proper and filthy at the same time. To be clear, she wasn't complaining about it. She just never thought the two would seamlessly blend so well.

The flick of his tongue against her swollen nub suppressed the air in her lungs while rendering her completely under his spell.

His coordinated assault with his mouth and his fingers had her hips bucking as she tried to get closer yet pull away from the unimaginable pleasure he gave to her.

He placed a firm hand across her waist, keeping her right where he wanted her.

"No, running, Treasure. Not until I get to feel you break apart on my tongue."

"For a king," she choked out through the waves of pleasure crashing over her, "your mouth is so damn nasty."

She could feel his smile burgeon against her mound, and she couldn't decide if it was disturbing or damn sexy that he was literally smiling against her clit.

"Oh, Treasure, if you think my mouth is filthy, just wait until you experience my sex."

He licked and sucked her flesh while sliding his fingers in and out of her, grazing against the knot of nerves, forcing her to the edge of release even if she wasn't ready to be there.

"Your Majesty, I'm…"

He pulled his mouth away from her, hovering over her as the intensity of his stare bore down on her. His eyes were searing with fire and filled with what looked like righteous anger.

"While it takes a certain amount hubris to don the crown, I am not so full of myself that I want my lovers to refer to me using a courtesy title. Hear me and hear me well. The only name I want to hear crossing your lips when my face is buried in your sex is Aléx."

He added another finger to the two already inside her, creating a glorious stretch that had her clamping down on his digits.

"To you, especially when we are like this—" he used his thumb to circle her clit, dragging another hungry moan from her "—I am always Aléx."

The hunger in his gaze was too raw. She tried to close her eyes and shield herself from him. She was so close, if he moved his fingers just the right way, she'd reach her peak.

"Look at me when I'm speaking to you."

He removed his fingers, lightly slapping them against her swollen clit. The sensation was surprisingly erotic, ramping up her arousal, but keeping her from coming at the same time.

She opened her eyes, finding a wicked gleam in his eyes.

"Oh, God," she mewled. That got her another slap against her clit, leaving her body strung so tightly with pleasure she was worried something in her might snap.

"No, not God." He swatted her nub again, but this time he followed that with a soothing strum of his fingertips against the sensitive flesh. "Aléx."

She nodded, quite frankly, because she couldn't find the focus to speak. Her climax was hovering over her just out of reach, and her entire body was aching for it. The truth was, she'd give this man anything he wanted, call him whatever he wanted if he'd let her orgasm right now.

It wasn't lost on her that he was certain of this information himself. Even if she hadn't come to that conclusion on her own, the diabolical gleam of satisfaction swimming in his gaze disabused her of any notion that Aléx wasn't completely aware of the power he held over her right now.

He slammed his mouth against hers, spreading her arousal between their lips, allowing her to taste herself on him.

"Whose fingers are you going to ride to completion?"

"Yours." The word was barely loud enough for him to hear if his face hadn't been so close to hers.

"Who is going to bury himself inside you and take you as rough as you can stand it?"

"Y-you," she stammered. "It's…you."

His fingers were playing her like a skilled musician's, knowing almost instinctively which note would complement the arrangement he was composing.

"And what…is…my…name?"

Her body, and mind for that matter, were no

longer under her control. She ached for release, and this man was the key to that. If she weren't naked with her legs spread wide without the slightest bit of shame, she'd tell the good king about himself. But right now, the only thing she wanted, needed, was to come, and she wasn't going to jeopardize that for a silly thing like her pride.

"Aléx…your name is… Aléx."

"Such a good girl deserves a reward."

He slid down her body again, resuming his position between her legs, latching on to her nub and suckling as if the secret elixir of life could be drawn from it. With a twist of his wrist, her body bowed as her orgasm crested, pulling her muscles taut, forcing her to clamp down on his fingers with abandon.

When her body finally relaxed, she fell limp, throwing her arm over her eyes as she tried to come to grips with the fact that a king she'd met for the first time in her life had given her the best orgasm she'd ever had.

"Oh no, Treasure." In the distance, she could hear the familiar sound of a wrapper being torn. "There's no rest for the weary. That was just an opening salvo."

His weight returning to the bed pulled her gaze to him in time to see the angry purple dome of his hardened length. His arousal had gone from impressive to mouthwatering, with its bulging red veins denoting just how much he wanted to be inside her.

Apparently, his filthy mouth had done more than just aid in her climax. It had amped up his need to what looked like an almost painful level.

She watched him slide the condom down over his length. He stalked over, leaning down and kissing her softly before he asked, "Are you still with me?"

He was sexy and thoughtful, checking in to make sure she was still all right with this.

This man cannot be real.

He started to pull away when she closed her hand over his length, stroking him from root to tip and reveling in the full-body shudder that she could feel passing through him.

"Yes, Aléx." She made a point of saying his name, feeling the raw heat of his need emanating from his body. "I'm more than ready for whatever you plan to dish out."

He parted her thighs, seating himself at her entrance, slowly pushing himself in.

Despite her eagerness for him after already experiencing such a fantastic orgasm, there was a definite sting as her body stretched to accommodate him.

Aléx placed a gentle kiss on her temple as he

softly whispered, "Shhh, Treasure. That's right. Be a good girl and take all of me."

She moaned, eagerly accepting him into her body.

Why this man's words and voice made her brain shut off and her body respond with such unapologetic acquiescence, she didn't know. What she did know was that when he finally bottomed out inside her and lightly raked his thumb against her clit, pleasure exploded inside her. Once again, she'd lost control of her body and willingly, enthusiastically ceded that control to him. He began to thrust in and out of her while she was still amid her climax, driving her higher, prolonging it until she was nearly ready to cry.

Throughout their passionate encounter, he kept pushing her beyond her limits, making her crave the way his powerful strokes pushed her closer to and through such earth-shattering climaxes that she was weak, and yet so needy for more.

There had never been anyone who knew her so well that it was almost as if they could reach inside her and pull her secret wants and needs from her and be so certain how to answer them. It was almost like he knew her. Like he saw her...the real her.

She held on to the bed posts for dear life, and

Aléx buried himself in her over and over from behind until she was spilling over into bliss again.

"Aléx," she cried out.

The sound of his name crossing her lips as both a plea and a prayer made him deepen his strokes, fusing them together in body and spirit.

"Say it again." He ground the words out through what sounded like his clenched jaw. Her face was buried in the plush pillow, so she couldn't swear to it.

"Aléx!" she screamed as she succumbed to the orgasm locking her muscles in place.

At the sound of her yelling his name, his grip on her hips tightened, his rhythm faltered, and he buried himself inside her one last time until his climax took hold of him. She could feel the throbbing pulse of his release as he emptied himself into the condom. When he collapsed against her, blanketing her with his strong form, she felt more cared for, more content, more herself, than she could remember in her recent years.

This was absolute heaven. As far as she was concerned, nothing could ruin this perfect moment.

Aléx rolled to his back, quickly disposing of the condom before pulling her into his arms.

And then the universe showed her why she should never tempt it to show her just how terrible it could be. Aléx said, "Good, God, Reigna.

How could I have gone all these years of seeing you at this gala, never knowing how fantastically we would fit together?"

Just like that, per usual where Regina was concerned, her sister Reigna had been hoisted into the spotlight, and Regina's place was in the background, if visible at all. This was the best sex of her life, and her lover thought she was her twin sister. Even in the most unlikely circumstances, Regina had ended up in her sister's shadow yet again.

CHAPTER THREE

Four months later...

ALÉX STARTED HIS day the same way he had every day for the last four months. He sat up in bed, fighting the urge to reach for the body he knew wouldn't be there. The same body he'd cursed at each new sunrise and ravaged in his dreams each night.

Once he'd forced himself to forget about how tantalizing those vivid dreams were and intentionally ignored how his body tightened at the memories he couldn't seem to let go, he made quick work of showering in ice-cold water.

"Damn it."

Aléx slammed his hand against the hard tile of the shower stall. He was fairly certain it was the finest marble on the market he was slamming his ringed hand against, and here he was treating it like it was a cheap piece of plastic that could be scratched without thought and replaced without much effort or cost.

This was not like him.

No matter that Aléx had grown up in opulent wealth. He'd always known that his lifestyle was a gift for his service, and he should never take it for granted. Yet since that night four months ago, he'd been holding on to his focus and his discipline with every ounce of his being, all because he couldn't forget her.

This also wasn't like him.

Aléx didn't pine over women. He used them for mutual pleasure, and when both parties were satisfied, he went back to his life of duty and service without a care. He wasn't cruel to women. He simply made sure he only ever slept with women who knew there would be no more beyond their mutual physical satisfaction.

As his mind began to replay that night for the millionth time, he ran a harsh hand through his wet hair, trying to figure out what was so special about this particular woman. She had him so desperate to taste her that he'd forgotten to give her his practiced "we only have tonight" speech that proceeded any sexual encounter he had with a partner.

A derisive laugh climbed up from his chest, spilling through his lips and echoing in the marble-and-glass stall. The joke was on him. He hadn't needed to give Reigna Devereaux that speech because she was gone as soon as he'd fallen into a sound sleep. And the next time he'd heard of her, he was receiving a royal wedding invitation announcing her as the Nyeusian king's bride.

How's that for turning the tables?

He should've been relieved that Reigna hadn't had designs on him. The fact that she'd so quickly married someone else should've made his year. Too bad the ugly mark of jealousy that clawed at him from the inside hadn't received the memo. As a result, he was still obsessing over her four months later.

Still disgusted with himself for being unable to shake whatever this thing inside him was that kept him fixated on the woman, he dressed and headed to breakfast in his office. Finding his plate waiting for him and the global news playing on the television reminded him what he was here to do.

He was here to take care of his people, not obsess over a single sexual encounter that happened four months ago.

He was just about to drink the piping hot black brew in his cup when he heard the news anchor say, "When a concrete princess from Brooklyn becomes the real-life queen of an exotic island paradise, you get a fairy tale come true. Viewers, please welcome one of Brooklyn's most famous daughters. She's formerly known as Reigna Devereaux of the Devereaux Inc. ilk. Now she is known as Her Majesty, Queen Reigna of Nyeusi. Oh, and her husband, King Jasiri, is joining her too."

Aléx's fist closed around the delicate china, and he had to force every muscle in his hand to relax so he wouldn't shatter the thing in his palm.

He thanked every deity he could remember for the foresight to put the cup on a level surface, because the sight of her on the television left him boneless, unable to move or do anything but watch her on the screen.

She wore a cocktail-length A-line dress with its high waist accented by a large belt. She was breathtaking, her full cheeks high as she greeted the anchor with a smile and an enthusiastic handshake. Seeing her form again made him lean toward the television, giving it and her his entire attention.

The camera angle widened, giving the viewing audience a full-body shot, and the floor beneath him might as well have opened and swallowed him. She was beyond royal. She was celestial in vibrant purple, gold, and black colors. They were woven into a beautiful African print, and the gold lioness broach on her collar highlighted her strength, grace and poise as she continued to walk across the stage.

He was losing himself in the way those colors complemented her beautiful, deep brown skin, producing a soft and inviting glow around her that called to him so strongly he nearly stood from his chair. But then a hint of something familiar plucked at the back of his mind until he realized why she wore those colors. They were the national colors of Nyeusi.

Jasiri's land.

Her husband's kingdom.

Had Aléx known Reigna and Jasiri had a past? Yes. According to the headlines, they'd been broken up for at least two years when she'd found her way into Aléx's bed. Reigna was a free agent, and her choosing to go back to her ex after a night with Aléx shouldn't have bothered him one bit. Irrationality aside, receiving their wedding invitation had pulled out a jealous possessiveness Aléx hadn't known himself capable of, and he'd been fighting it every day of the last four months.

Regret and anger mixed in his gut, creating a toxic concoction that was probably going to give him an ulcer if he didn't get the rage spreading through his system under control. And there, just as his vision began to cloud with red, he saw Jasiri's hand touch hers, guiding her to the sofa where the hosts of the news show sat.

How had he missed the man? The answer to that was simple. Reigna. She was all he'd seen or focused on since he'd heard her name announced.

The host went on to fawn over Reigna. Even though Jasiri was at her side, it was clear Reigna was the star of the show. Honestly, it was fitting. No one compared to the sultry, strong and caring woman who'd set his body on fire.

Aléx tried to focus on just her, to ignore Jasiri's presence, but he couldn't. Because slowly he began to see that Reigna wasn't a separate entity. She was with Jasiri. Not just married to him, connected to him.

Aléx could see the way she glanced up to Jasiri, the way she sought his hand or his arm whenever more than a few moments passed without the couple touching. It was there for anyone looking to see. She adored her husband.

He waited for the jealousy he'd been harboring since he'd declined the invitation to their Nyeusian royal wedding to flash hot in his blood. But as he watched their exchanges, he understood they were truly in love.

Whatever the thing was that had had Aléx in such an unbreakable hold for these last four months, it didn't so much as simmer within him. It wasn't just quiet. It was gone.

He pulled his eyes away from the screen, trying to focus on his own thoughts. Reigna was in love with Jasiri. As much as he wanted to be angry about that, as much as he couldn't stand that Jasiri had one-upped him, Aléx couldn't begrudge the two the obvious connection they shared.

He was just ready to change the channel literally and figuratively when Reigna said, "We're happy to announce we're expecting our first child." She placed a loving hand against the bottom of her stomach, display a slight bump that had been concealed by the silhouette of her dress. "I'm four months along."

Cold spilled down Aléx's spine as he did the mental math in his head. It had been four months since the night they'd shared. Four months since he'd lost himself inside her.

Yes, he'd worn a condom. But he knew from personal experience that condoms didn't always work.

There was a crack in the door he'd kept soundly shut around his heart. He took in a noisy breath that was equal parts pain and joy. Could this be his baby? Could he be a father again?

And as he watched Jasiri place a possessive hand on Reigna's stomach, that anger he'd thought he'd lost came roaring back to life like a powerful flood slamming against his chest, making it almost impossible to breathe.

"So help me, Reigna," he growled through clenched teeth. "If you'd stoop low enough to try to pass my baby off as Jasiri's, you'd better prepare yourself for a battle. Because I'm coming, and I'm bringing hell with me."

Aléx stood in front of the floor-to-ceiling window that made up the fourth wall in the conference room of Gemini Queens, Reigna's cosmetics company. He'd had few direct dealings with her with respect to commerce. He had people to handle the dirty details of business. There was no reason for him to have muddied the waters in that respect.

His pulse beat loudly in his ears as he waited for Reigna to join him for what she believed was a matter of her company's business dealings with his country.

They had business to deal with, certainly. But it didn't have a damn thing to do with commerce.

"Your Majesty, thank you so much for stopping by to speak with me while we're both in town."

He turned around, bracing himself for seeing her in person after their last time together. Unbridled anger raced through his vessels like poison when he thought of what she might have done. But he also feared the tangible chemistry that had put them in this situation to begin with might be there too.

When he laid eyes on her in a fitted knee-length dress, her bump just beginning to show and all her curves on display, attraction never made an appearance.

He shook his head, not understanding what was going on inside him. He'd obsessed over this woman for months. Now, except for the notion that she might be the mother of his child, there was nothing there between them.

She smiled and offered her hand to him. He didn't take it. He was so busy trying to figure out what the hell was going on, touching her seemed unwise.

"Reigna, let us dispense with the niceties of royals meeting. I think you know why I'm here, and things will work out best for everyone involved if you're honest with me."

"I'm not sure what you're referring to, King Aléxandros."

That was the second time she'd called him by his title, and it stirred something in him as he remembered her spread out beneath him, wild with pleasure as he forbade her from calling him anything other than his name.

It was on the tip of his tongue to correct her. But as he looked at her, the pull of fire and need that had been there before wasn't now.

"Then I'll be blunt." She lifted her eyes in anticipation of Aléxandros's next words. "Am I the father of the baby you're carrying, and are you attempting to pass it off as your husband's?"

Her jaw dropped, and her brown eyes turned to steel as she gazed at him. She took a step back and moved her hand to her wrist, where her smartwatch rested elegantly against her skin. He grabbed her arm, preventing her from touching what he was certain was some kind of security alarm.

"Uh-uh, Queen Reigna. I've got one of those too. Let's say we settle this before you bring in the cavalry. Is it possible I'm the father of the child you're carrying?"

She snatched her arm from him, anger burning in her gaze as she put distance between them.

"Who the hell do you think you are, asking me something like that?"

His jaw tightened, making him worry that he might crack the bones there as he pried it open to speak.

"I'm the man you begged to pleasure you exactly four months ago. So I'll ask again. Am I the father of your child?"

Something sparked in her eyes that he couldn't quite make out. She tilted her head, staring at him as if she was understanding something he wasn't privy to.

"King Aléxandros, considering my husband is a dark-skinned Black man and you're of European descent, I think it would be pretty stupid of me to try to pass your baby off as Jasiri's. This is not your baby."

Her gaze was steady and her voice calm. Everything about the way she stared at him painted her as the picture of poise and virtue. Everything in her countenance said she was telling him the truth. But the familiar darkness he'd fought so hard to bury in his past wouldn't let this small kernel of hope die.

Not again...not this time.

"Forgive me if I don't take the word of the woman who went from one king's bed to another with such apparent ease."

She folded her arms as she leaned to one side, jutting out one hip.

"I'm not going to be too many more liars and whores, no matter how prettily you dress up your words. I've answered your question. Now get out, before I cause an international incident and throw you out on your ass."

He knew he was out of line with his insinuations, but the need to know wouldn't let him curb his tongue.

"This won't be the last you've heard from me, Queen Reigna. If I must sic my lawyers on you and your king to establish paternity, I have no problems with the inevitable scandal that will follow. I don't think your newly installed king can say the same."

With that, he took his leave. Reigna Devereaux might have Jasiri wrapped around her finger, but she didn't hold any power over Aléx...not anymore. If he had to fight for his child, he would. Never again would someone take a child from him without him battling tooth and nail with blood and bone. If Reigna's child was his, he'd go to hell and back to claim it.

CHAPTER FOUR

"Heifer, did you sleep with King Aléxandros when you were at the commerce gala on Obsidian Island?"

Regina pulled the phone away from her ear to look at the screen as if her sister could see the shock on her face.

"Ahhh, yeah. I did. How do you know about that?"

Regina and her twin sister Reigna were close, but not so close that Regina would share the details of her sex life with her. Especially when she was too embarrassed because her sex partner thought he'd been screwing the popular twin instead of her.

"Because he ambushed me in the Gemini Queens' conference room, demanding to know if the baby I'm carrying is his. I cannot believe you let this happen."

Reigna's voice jumped across the phone line, delivering a metaphorical slap upside the head that Regina nearly physically tried to dodge.

"Listen, you were the one who asked me to pretend to be you at that stupid gala in the first place."

Regina knew it was a silly argument. She sounded like she'd barely made it out of elementary school instead of having a whole Ph.D.

"Regina." The hard way her sister called her name made a chill spill down Regina's spine. By all accounts, she was the serious twin, and Reigna was the fun one. When Reigna got serious, things were bad…really bad.

"Regina," her sister said again. "I didn't tell you to sleep with that man while pretending to be me. He's threatening lawyers. Nyeusi cannot afford a scandal. There cannot be even a sliver of doubt that I'm carrying the next rightful monarch of the House of Adebesi. You'd better fix this and do it fast. I found out where he's staying. I'm texting you the address now. Get up off your ass and make this right."

Her messenger app dinged, alerting her to the new text from her sister. Before she could pull the phone from her face to look at it, she heard the click of the line ending the call. Damn, if her sister hung up on her without saying goodbye, then Reigna was pissed off.

Her sister was right. It was time for Regina to grow a backbone and come clean with Aléx. She'd hoped the Atlantic Ocean would've been wide enough that she'd never have to see him again and deal with this. Just like always, her luck was trash, and yet again, the universe was denying her what she wanted.

Four months ago, she'd wanted to stay snuggled up with Aléx in his hotel room. That man had delivered the best sex of her life, and walking away from that while her body still ached from all the things he'd done to her was the hardest thing she'd ever had to do. She might've stayed if Aléx hadn't called Regina by her sister's name, pulling her back into reality, where she knew that moment could never be extended into more. How could it be? He thought he'd slept with her identical twin. There was no way she could explain the twin swap thing to him and have him meet her with anything but rejection.

That's what she'd told herself for the first couple of months, that he'd never understand. Once Reigna and Jasiri's marriage became public, there was too much at stake for her to attempt to reach out to Aléx. The Nyeusian monarchy couldn't afford the scandal, and the Nyeusian people would suffer for Regina's selfishness. She couldn't allow that to happen, so she did the only thing she could do: she swallowed her wants and buried herself in her work to forget.

There was only one problem.

She hadn't forgotten.

* * *

Aléx's large steps ate up the plush carpet as he headed toward the door. Reigna had finally come to her senses, and she'd come to address the predicament they found themselves in. He was relieved she hadn't attempted to ignore him. If she was here, maybe, just maybe, she was willing to work this out amicably so they could come together and do what was best for the child.

If that's your child.

He pushed his thoughts away, back into the recesses of his mind. He couldn't handle that prospect. Not after the small sliver of hope had pierced his heart and made him want what he'd lost so long ago.

He shook his head and straightened his shoulders, stepping into his king's persona.

"Queen Reigna," he began as he opened the door. "It seems once again we find ourselves in my hotel—"

Aléx's jaw dropped as he looked at the woman before him. She had the same build, the same face as the woman he'd spoken to earlier today. But with her cropped T-shirt exposing her soft stomach, he knew this was not the woman he'd crossed swords with earlier today.

"Oh my God, you're not her."

The woman shook her head as she stepped past him and into the room. She waited for him to close the door behind him. Once he had, she gave him a shaky smile.

"Hello, Your Majesty... I'm Regina Devereaux, Reigna's identical twin sister, and the woman you slept with four months ago."

The shock of her words turned his blood to ice, hardening him from the inside out, making it impossible for him to speak.

A twin?

She was a twin?

His mouth hung open in disbelief as his eyes poured over her, looking for a sign that this was some sort of joke.

The same dark eyes he'd connected with when she'd swooped in to rescue him from unwanted female attention stared back at him. Even now they were filled with compassion and concern for him.

That spark of worry he saw floating in her gaze scraped across his soul, igniting a blaze of anger that threatened to overcome him.

He fisted his hands at his sides as if he were physically trying to wrestle his rising anger under his control. He was a king. Control was kind of his thing. Losing it could mean the difference between life and death and between the success and failure of his nation, his people. He had to keep his head on straight.

"What type of game are you and your sister playing at?"

His jaw clicked with each word. He was certain it would ache later, considering how tightly he was clenching his teeth. He tightened the muscles there even more, knowing it was either deal with a sore jaw or put his fist through the wall of a hotel he didn't own in a country he didn't rule.

She stepped closer to him. He was sure she could see the fury humming off him in waves, but she kept walking until she was directly in front of him, as if she welcomed his anger, accepted it. He reasoned either she had no sense of self-preservation, or she was out of her mind. His anger was at a raging boil now; he was certain he could rip her to shreds with his bare hands.

Then the soft scent of roses and vanilla filled his senses, acting like a soothing balm, dousing his rage even though he wanted nothing more than to pour gasoline on it.

"Your Majesty."

"Aléx!" He bellowed. "To you, I am always Aléx. Don't make me repeat myself."

He didn't know why her use of his courtesy title raised his hackles so much. People used it repeatedly throughout any given day when addressing him. And yet it sounded so wrong crossing those full lips. Lips he'd tasted, lips he'd devoured, and heaven help him, even in his anger, he wanted to devour again.

"Aléx... I... I didn't mean to deceive you."

"You sure about that, Treasure? Because I've spent the last four months thinking I slept with your sister and not you. If that's not deception, I don't know what is."

He expected her to cower at his words. That's what most people did when they earned his displeasure. But not this woman. She stood bold before him, owning the disdain he was so generously dishing out.

She held his gaze, as true and as strong as it had been that night four months ago. Again, it soothed him, making him want to forget even when he needed to remember.

"I never intended to say more than hello and goodbye to anyone that night. Reigna and Jasiri were secretly married in a civil ceremony at the Nyeusian embassy here in America, and she was off in Nyeusi helping Jasiri secure his throne. That's the only reason I was there in the first place."

His eyes narrowed into slits as he watched her try to make sense out of the nonsensical.

"What does any of this have to do with you crawling into my bed and letting me think I was sleeping with your sister?"

To her credit, she didn't falter. Her gaze remained steady on him, and he couldn't help but be impressed by whatever it was that was driving her to face him and his wrath.

"Reigna's absence would've been noticed at an event of that social and business magnitude. The press would've begun digging, and Jasiri's Uncle Pili would've thwarted their plans and possibly stolen the throne away from Jasiri. Besides that, it would've been bad for Gemini Queens if the face of the company didn't turn up. I was only supposed to show my face, smile and mingle. But when I saw that woman pawing at you, I knew I had to do something."

Her forthrightness threw him. How could she be so calm as she recounted her wrongdoing?

"I wasn't expecting to end up in your bed, Aléx. It all just sort of happened. One minute we were talking, and the next we were all over each other."

They certainly had been. He could still feel the heat of her burning flesh against his, still feel the need that vibrated through her body every time he touched her.

She was so close to him, his fingers ached to touch her. Although he knew he couldn't give in to that desire, it still spread through his veins like an opiate, making every ounce of his being crave her from the first and only taste he'd had of her.

He turned, spotting the desk behind them. He

leaned over it, pressing his knuckles into its cool wood surface. He hoped the bite of the wood against his flesh would sober that temptation. The discomfort was supposed to keep him focused instead of making him want to reach out and possess her the same way he had four months ago.

"I was trying to protect my sister, Aléx. That night with you was an unexpected gift I had no way of anticipating."

He chuckled at her use of the word *gift*. He straightened as the heat of his anger began to swell again.

"Funny how I'd thought of it that way too until I thought you were trying to pass my baby off as Jasiri's."

Yes, this…this rage, this searing, ugly thing that made him want to lash out, *that* he could hold on to. He turned and closed the distance between them again.

"Until you walked into this room obviously not pregnant, tore open a familiar hole in my—"

He clasped his jaw shut, refusing to let the rest of that sentence find its way into the ether. That was his alone. He wouldn't share it with anyone else. Not now. Not ever.

The fire flashing in Aléx's eyes turned from fury to pain. Sharp pain that seemed to stab at something vital inside him, robbing him of breath. Fear for him, not of him, pushed her forward, making her grip his forearm.

"Aléx, are you okay?"

He didn't respond; he simply stared at his arm where they were joined as if it was some mystical puzzle he was trying to complete or unlock.

What the hell was going on? He was a king, for goodness' sake. If she'd broken him with this little twin swap stunt, Reigna was going to kill her. Having this king drop dead of shock because of something she did would haunt Regina for the rest of her life. She had to fix this.

"Aléx, please," she begged frantically. "What is it? What can I do?"

A dark focus crystalized in his eyes as he shifted his arm until he shook her hand free and clasped her wrist in his painful grip.

He pulled her so close that her body was flush against his. She could feel the hard drum of his heart pounding through his chest. She wanted to flatten her hand against it, try to soothe him until she could see reason slip into his expression again. But he kept her to him, keeping her wrist in his unyielding grip so she could do nothing but stand there looking up into his fiery blue gaze.

It should've frightened her. It should've had every one of her danger bells going off in her head. But fear wasn't what she was feeling. No, deep in the pit of her belly, desire flickered from a small spark to a full-on inferno. There was no fear. There was only need. The same need that had found her in his bed, beneath him, begging for every filthy thing he'd done for her, to her. She melted against him, hanging on to every sliver of emotion she saw play across his face.

Beneath the obvious anger, there was that same need she felt burning through her system. The flush running just beneath his skin was the same as the night he'd taken her to unimaginable heights in his bed. Yes, she was here for another round of that, even if it was because he was so furious with her that devouring her was the only way he could temper his anger.

Too needy to be patient, she licked her dry lips and opened her mouth to speak.

"What can I do, Aléx?"

His lips turned up at the corners, giving his classically handsome features a sinister twist.

"You can start by making up for the little trick you played on me by marrying me and giving me the child you owe me."

Well damn. Of all the things she'd expected— no—wanted to hear from him, it sure as hell wasn't that.

CHAPTER FIVE

"Say what now?"

He watched confusion clear out the lust he'd previously seen in her eyes.

She'd wanted him. He was certain of it, because the same ache that had her licking her full lips had his heart racing inside his chest. But then the ache that had threatened to swallow him whole four months ago tried to crawl its way out of the dank grave he'd buried it in. Instead of leaning into need, he'd lashed out by saying the most unhinged thing he could think of.

But now that he'd said it, he wouldn't take it back.

"You owe me a child, and in order for me to have a child, I must be married due to legitimacy laws concerning the line of succession. That means you're going to marry me and give me what I'm owed."

"What you're owed? You seriously think I owe you a baby because you jumped to conclusions about my sister's pregnancy?"

She was right. He had jumped to conclusions. That didn't matter as far as he was concerned. He would not take fault in this. Not one single iota of it.

"The bill's come due for the little game you and your sister played. I've come to collect, and you have to give me what I'm owed."

As the last syllable of his sentence left his mouth, her left brow rose as she pointed her forefinger at her chest.

"I don't have to do anything but stay Black and die."

Her words short-circuited his brain, disrupting the anger and lust that had clouded his senses since she'd walked into his hotel room announcing that he'd slept with the wrong twin.

He tilted his head, taking her in. Her round hip was jutted out to one side, and her face, usually bright with sass and snark, was pulled into tight lines. All the softness her curves held was now replaced with stern rigidness that let him know Regina Devereaux was no pushover.

Everything in her stance said she was going to fight him on this. That was okay. He was a king. He was used to waging war to get what he wanted. Regina Devereaux would fall prey to his will the way everyone else did.

On its face, his request was obviously ludicrous. Even he wasn't so far gone in this moment that he couldn't see that. Unfortunately, the empty hole in his heart that had been sitting there for five years had shrunk enough for him to notice when there was a chance that he was going to become a father. God help him, after feeling hope for the first time in too many years, he couldn't simply walk away from it just because this was all some cruel twist of fate.

He was a king. He made his own fate. He would be a father again. Making that happen depended on his ability to convince this woman he wasn't as unbalanced as he sounded.

"I have absolutely no idea what that means." He shook his head and stepped toward her. "What I do know is that I want a child, and you're going to give me one."

"People in hell want ice water, but they're still hot and thirsty. I'm not giving you a damn thing. Not even the time of day. Goodbye, King Aléxandros."

She turned toward the door, and he stepped in front of her, halting her forward motion.

"We're not done yet."

"We absolutely are done. You cannot force someone to marry you and have a child with you. Just because you're a king doesn't mean you can just command people to do whatever you want."

He shrugged. "Actually, it kind of does."

That comment took some of the steam out of

her stance. He knew he'd made a chink in her armor when he saw one side of her mouth begrudgingly lift into a small smile.

"You are so insufferable. Is that also part of being a king?"

He nodded, taking another cautious step to her. When she didn't bolt, he ushered her over to the large sofa in the center of the room and bade her to take a seat next to him.

"What kind of man goes around demanding a woman marry him and give him a baby? You know nothing about me. Why would you want to tie yourself to me like that? We don't love each other. How could you consider marrying someone you don't know if you like, let alone love?"

He sat down, extending his arm against the back of the couch and crossing his legs. As he relaxed, so did she. He liked that she took her cues from him. Her willingness to follow his lead had gifted him unimaginable pleasure. If he could only convince her to follow his desires in this matter, maybe he could find something else. Peace.

"Regina, this would be a marriage of convenience, not love. Love is messy and unstable, and when it goes bad, it can poison everything. It can be weaponized, and when it strikes a blow, it can kill you as dead as any bullet."

If anyone understood that, it would be him.

What happened five years ago had taught him a very slow and painful lesson about love. It nearly killed him, and his resuscitation from it hadn't left him unscarred or unchanged.

"As the king, my number one concern is to simultaneously uphold the monarchy while serving my citizens. Choosing a consort comes down to a few things. Trust, the willingness to provide support to the sovereign, and compatibility in the ways that are important to each party."

"You said trust is a must." Her words were quick and sharp as if she were trying to get them all out at once. "Knowing that the only reason we're in this mess now is because I lied to you, how on earth can you trust me enough to be such an important part of your life?"

He waited to see if she was going to say more and found her rapt attention zeroed in on him, waiting for an answer to her question. If she was waiting that intently, he had to hope that somewhere deep down, she was considering his proposal.

"Yes, you lied. But before that, you interjected yourself into a situation to help a man who was a total stranger to you. That tells me you're strong and compassionate. Those are two qualities that aren't necessarily in abundance when it comes to wealthy people. Your actions, much more than your words, tell me I can trust you to do what's right when necessary. It was also proof that you'd be willing to support me as I support the nation. Lastly, if Reigna is the face of your company, I know that you're the brilliant sister who works science like it's magic in her lab. That's a beautiful mix of qualities that I couldn't buy with all the money and power at my disposal."

Her shoulders sank as she leaned into the cushions. Her gaze was still furtive as it flitted across him. But she was at least listening to him.

"Aléx, this makes not one bit of sense. Why would you even consider marrying and having a child with a complete stranger?"

"As I said before, I'm a king, Regina. My duty is to produce an heir so that the line of succession can continue. That heir must be legitimate, so marriage is also my duty. There's no one in my circle that I trust enough to contemplate having a child with. As I'm sure your sister can tell you, the royal court can be a pit of vipers waiting for an opportunity to strike. And I'm thirty-seven."

"Hey," she interrupted him. "That's only three years older than me. You say that like thirty-seven is ancient."

Her offense was noted by the wrinkling of her nose, making him chuckle. "In my world, that *is* ancient for a sitting king to be without an heir. If I must have a child, I'd like it to be with someone who at least understands what kindness and compassion are."

She closed her eyes as if she were trying to conceal something from him. He had no right to it. He had no right to her. But the selfish king in him wanted all her secrets. In his world, secrets were power. With Regina, though, he didn't want to use them against her. He simply wanted to unburden her of whatever darkness her thoughts were cloaking her in.

"Is it that you don't want children?"

She shook her head, looking away in the distance before bringing her gaze back to him.

"I'm the twin who planned her imaginary wedding and how many imaginary kids she and her imaginary husband would have. I even named all three of them. Reigna wanted nothing to do with a future family and children. Fate's funny like that. It gives the very thing you've always ached for to people who never wanted it."

Was that resentment? Did she envy her sister's life?

The thought of Regina pining for something she couldn't have tightened an invisible knot in his chest. In his bed, he'd given her everything she desired. And as he watched her push down this apparent desire of hers, he ached to give her this too.

He hardly knew her. Until today, he hadn't

even known her real name. Yet when her soft, sad eyes met his, he was certain she'd shared the important parts of herself when they'd met in his country.

"We can make our own fate, Regina. All it would take is you saying yes, and we can make it happen together."

Her mouth opened slightly, and he could see the yes taking shape on her lips when a shrill ringing sound disturbed the moment.

Regina shook her head, pulling her phone from her pocket. "This is my sister. I've gotta go."

She stood up, quickly hurrying toward the door.

"What about my proposition, Regina?"

"What about it? It's the most absurd thing anyone has ever said to me. No, I will not marry you and have your baby. This isn't some sort of rom-com where two quirky strangers agree to something this ridiculous and it all works out. Life doesn't work that way. My life doesn't work that way."

She yanked the door open and ran into the hallway, leaving him to watch her retreat to safety.

As he watched the elevator doors close, he smiled.

"You can run, Regina…for now."

Regina went directly home from Aléx's hotel. She knew she should've gone back to her sister's, but she was too raw to do it. Aléx's proposal, on its face, was unthinkable. There was no way she could agree to marry this man and have his child. He was a king. This wasn't how monarchies worked, was it? Wasn't there some sort of vetting process when it came to becoming a monarch's intended? It couldn't be as simple as a handshake and a deal. Could it?

She shook her head as she stepped off the elevator and walked to the door of her penthouse apartment. Her brain was firing on all cylinders as it tried to make sense of Aléx's proposal. No matter how she tried, there was no sense to be made, and so she did the next best thing. She dropped her things on the front table, grabbed her iPad Pro off the charging dock she'd left it on this morning, and sat down in her armchair with all the fluffy pillows a scientist could want.

Calm began to settle in her mind and in her bones as she twirled the Apple Pencil now in her hand. She drew a tightly coiled strand of African American hair, attaching notes on the opposite side of the image on what Black hair needs to thrive.

Moisture retention
Gentle yet effective cleansing
Deep conditioning with effective detangling

Styling products that provide moisture but don't weigh the hair down
Styling products that decrease frizz, provide hold, and prevent dryness and breakage
Gentle fragrance

She continued jotting notes down, getting lost in her work, trying her best to ignore the ache that had flared up inside her since Aléx made his offer. Having a family had always been a priority for Regina. It was probably selfish, considering how terrible her parents were at loving Regina and her sister. What made her confident she wouldn't ruin a child the way her parents had almost ruined her?

A different ache in her chest blossomed as the warmth of love and the bitterness of grief commingled like never-ending vines. Ace Devereaux, her great-uncle, the man who had taught both Regina and Reigna what it felt like to be loved. That man had swept in and filled those two affection-starved little girls with so much love, at times they'd thought they might burst from it. That abundance of love was what lit the fire inside her to love her future children that way. Her ultimate dream had been to have a child while Ace was still with them, allow him to see how powerful his love had been. That hadn't been in God's plan, however. He'd called Ace home six months earlier.

Losing Ace had ripped a hole in her soul. And since he'd been gone, that ache for a family of her own had begun to resurface. Once Reigna had announced her pregnancy, the thought wouldn't turn her loose.

She took a breath, forcing her thoughts back onto the work in front of her. Life didn't give her what she wanted. It never had; there was no reason to think if she reached for what she wanted now, it would finally come true.

Defeated, she laid the tablet down on the coffee table next to her and pulled her phone from her pocket to call her sister. Better to get this over with now or her sister would more than likely wake her up at the ass crack of dawn for a follow-up on her conversation with Aléx.

"How did it go?"

No hello or greeting of any kind: her sister just got straight to the point. It was a clear sign that she'd reached her limit when it came to patience. Regina couldn't blame her. It wasn't every day that one twin's poor judgment could lead to actual war between two countries.

"I told him the truth. He wasn't happy about it, but he accepted it. He now knows there's no possible way that he fathered your baby."

Her sister was quiet as she took in Regina's

words, as if she were letting the relief bleed through her. Her problems were over now. Too bad Regina couldn't say the same.

"He's an obnoxious ass. Did he say or do anything to you that's gonna make me want to pop him in his mouth the next time I see him?"

Regina took comfort in knowing her sister would still defend her, even though it was Regina's fault they'd ended up in this mess to begin with.

"Like I said, he was upset. But he wasn't mean."

"That bastard is always mean. Every time I attended one of his galas, he pretty much just scowled the entire time, barely sparing a kind word for any of the vendors that bring revenue to his country." Reigna's words scraped against Regina's nerves, and she couldn't tell why. It wasn't like she and Aléx were besties. But somehow, she still felt the need to defend him.

"Not to me," Regina offered. "He's always been genuine and kind to me."

"If you say so," Reigna huffed. "Just know I don't believe you."

Her sister's dismissive tone continued to rub something raw inside Regina.

"If he were being mean, would he ask to keep seeing me?"

That wasn't exactly what he'd asked. But there was no way she was telling Reigna the real request Aléx had made of her.

"And you told him to go to hell, right?"

Irritation swelled up inside Regina, instantly putting her on the defensive.

"Why would I say no without even considering his request? He's handsome, charismatic, and a whole-ass king who is good in bed. Why would I dismiss him?"

"Regina." The way her sister said her name had Regina perched at the edge of her seat, ready to pounce, even though she was in the apartment alone. It was condescending to say the least. The expectation that Regina would do whatever Reigna had said, simply because the older twin had said it, made her eye twitch. Even worse than that, Regina usually did give in. Not because she felt she had to, but because she knew Reigna needed to feel like she was protecting her sister. It was a remnant of being ignored by their parents. In every situation, Reigna always had to center herself to feel seen.

Usually, Regina went along to get along. Tonight, that wasn't happening.

"What exactly are you trying to say, Reigna?"

"I'm saying," her sister began, "the man only wanted you because he thought you were me. Why on earth would you want to see him, knowing that?"

Anger swept through Regina, making her hand tighten against her iPhone. She squeezed it so hard she'd be surprised if there wasn't a crack across the screen by the time this conversation was done.

"So, you're the only twin that can pull a king? Is that what you're saying? Because there's no way a man as fine and refined as Aléx could possibly want your slacking twin, right?"

"Regina." Reigna's voice was soft, filled with concern, and that pissed her off even more. She knew her sister wasn't saying this to be cruel. She truly believed she was trying to spare her feelings. "That's not what I meant. Aléx couldn't lick your Jimmy Choos. I just don't like the idea that he could be using you to fulfill some sort of sick twin fantasy he has in his head. That's why I think it best you stay away from him."

Knowing her sister was concerned for her didn't subdue Regina's anger. Instead, it blazed as if she'd thrown gasoline on it.

"Well," Regina spat out. "It's a good thing I'm just as grown as you, and I don't need you to make decisions for me. Whether I decide to continue seeing Aléx or not is on me. So if I'm just the knockoff he's using to warm his bed, I guess that's on me too."

She ended the call and was about to throw her phone on the table when she saw the number from her doorman's station flash across the screen.

"Ms. Devereaux."

"Yes?" Her voice was sharp. She could hear his surprised intake of breath on the other end of the phone, and she mentally reprimanded herself. Poor Mr. Aires didn't deserve her taking out her anger with her sister out on him. Realizing her mistake, she took a breath and tried again. "What can I do for you, Mr. Aires?"

"Ma'am, there's a gentleman down here by the name of Aléx. He's got a bit of an entourage. Is it okay if I let him up?"

Of course, the subject of her argument with her sister would show up. Because that's just how life worked for her. When things were bad, life could always find a way to make things worse for Regina. Tempted to say no, she imagined the headlines in tomorrow's gossip rags. "*Concrete Princess Shuts Out King Charming.* Read page two for details."

Deciding she didn't need that kind of headache, she said, "Let him up, Mr. Aires."

CHAPTER SIX

ALÉX TAPPED LIGHTLY on the apartment door, slightly perturbed that she hadn't been standing there waiting to welcome him. She'd given her permission for him to be let in. Why play this game? There was only one reason: she was trying to exert her dominance in this situation. Too bad for her that domination had nothing to do with this situation. Outside of when they were in bed, he wanted a partner more than anything else. If they were going to make this happen, it had to be as a unit.

He might hold all the political power as king of Obsidian Island. However, for the kingdom to thrive, it took a concerted effort from the monarch and their consort to keep the country running. She had to understand that.

When he heard the door opening, he braced himself to tell her exactly that. Unfortunately, that thought flew out of his head once he saw her face.

Tight lines were etched into her forehead, her

jaw, and her mouth. When he looked into her red eyes, they were brimming with unshed tears. Every fiber of his being stretched taut, demanding he pull her into his arms and protect her from whatever had her so upset. Even if that whatever was him.

He moved to step inside her door when one of his security men laid a cautionary hand on his forearm.

"Your Majesty. We need to check the perimeter before you walk inside."

He leveled his gaze at Hugo, the head of his security team. He was a burly man, whose bulk had come in handy in protecting Aléx in one or two unsavory jams he'd found himself in. But tonight, Aléx didn't have time for protocol. Something was wrong with Regina, and she would never tell him what it was with his security team treating her like a potential threat to him in her own home.

Hugo gave an understanding nod and dropped his hand from Aléx's forearm. With the restraint gone, Aléx stepped inside. Before she could ask if his men were coming in, he closed the door and cupped her jaw gently.

The feel of her skin beneath his again transported him back to their one night together four months ago. A resulting fire flickered in his belly, but he refused to acknowledge it because this wasn't the time. Something was wrong, and he needed to know what it was. How could he fix it if he didn't know what she was facing?

"Treasure, what's wrong?"

She tried to shake her head, but he slipped his hand down, placing firm fingers against the back of her neck to keep her eyes focused on him.

"Don't lie to me, Regina. What has you so upset?"

She swallowed, closed her eyes, and took a steadying breath before she set her glassy eyes on him. The shimmer of her unshed tears made the rich brown of her irises sparkle.

"It's silly," she muttered. "I just had a fight with my sister. She's none too pleased with this situation I've created."

He scanned her eyes again, trying to get to the bottom of this. Regina's strong countenance was gone. Instead, hurt vibrated through her, from her inability to hold his gaze to the way she held herself with protective arms. The twins hadn't just argued. Whatever Reigna said had hurt Regina to the point that she was shaken, worn.

He dropped his hand from her neck and removed his suit jacket, tossing it on the long sofa behind him. He rolled up the sleeves of his white button-down shirt and reached for her hand.

"Where's your bedroom?"

Regina raised a questioning brow, making the corner of his mouth lift in amusement.

"Not for that, Regina. Whenever I was emotionally wrought as a child, my mother used to run me a bath and let me soak until all the tension of my harried feelings washed away with the water. Then she'd tuck me in and lie next to me until I was ready to talk. It's a practice I still use to this day. Whenever being king is too much, I take a soak, then go lie down to gain perspective on my thoughts and feelings. I'd like to do that for you...if you'd allow me to."

She studied him. Whatever she was looking for in his expression, she must have found it, because her lips curved into a soft smile before she said, "Down the hallway, last door on the right."

He gave her hand a reassuring squeeze before he followed her directions.

He didn't take time to appreciate the decor or even notice where anything was. Once she pointed him in the direction of her en suite bathroom, he set about his task.

He gave the room a brief glance before he spotted the large black hot tub with several decorative glass containers of different bath salts. He skimmed their labels until he found the lavender he was looking for.

When the tub was ready, he walked out of the bathroom in time to see her exit what appeared to be her walk-in closet in a red silk robe that fell to her mid-thigh. His body instantly tightened at the thought of what that robe was barely covering.

When she headed toward the bathroom, he cautioned himself not to look as she passed, because he knew what would happen the moment he saw that rich dark skin of the back of her thigh.

He was an admitted fool, however. Just as she passed him, his gaze dropped, and his cock went from twitching to semihard.

He pulled his gaze away just as she closed the door behind her, and thank goodness she had. If he'd listened to his body, he'd have followed her into that bath.

Giving himself a mental reprimand for not having better control over his body's reaction to her, he sat down on the foot bench of her king-size bed.

Think of financial reports, security council meeting minutes, lobbyist pitches, anything to get your body under control.

Eventually, the thought of dry reports calmed his body down, and he was able to make himself presentable.

When he looked up again, Regina was coming out of the bathroom. Now she was wearing a black camisole set with tiny silk shorts that instantly did away with all the hard mental work he'd done to make himself soft.

"So, what now?"

He was tempted to answer her question by lifting her up so that her thick legs wrapped around his waist, and he could devour her mouth while walking them to her rather large and convenient bed. Ultimately, he ignored his hardening length's demands and stood. He quickly pulled the linens back, taking her hand and pulling her to the bed.

He meant to step aside and bid her good-night, but she scooted to the other side of the bed, leaving space for him as her eyes, soft with sleep, silently pleaded for him to join her.

You are such a glutton for punishment.

He was, but how could he be expected to deny her anything she wanted when she begged so prettily it literally unlocked something in him that made him fulfill her wishes, even if he didn't intend to?

God help him if she ever learned she had that kind of power over him. It could signal all kinds of dangers for him. Ignoring the warning bells in his head, he removed one wing tip shoe and then the other before crawling into the bed beside her.

He pulled her back to him, her ass notching perfectly into his lap as he engulfed her in his arms, completely spooning her.

A relieved sigh escaped her lips. He could hear the emotional fatigue.

He placed a kiss on the top of her head and tightened his hold as he said, "Sleep."

She chucked. "How am I supposed to sleep with that thing poking me in the backside?"

He tightened his embrace again, adjusting his head so that he was smiling against the shell of her ear.

"It's a rather inconvenient consequence of being this close to you. Whenever you're near, my body seems to have a mind of its own, and you're the only thing it wants to focus on."

He felt her go stiff in his arms. Had he gone too far? Had he made her uncomfortable? He turned her, forcing her to face him. He was learning that Regina was good at hiding what she felt, except for when her eyes were on him. It was the only time she allowed him to break through her defenses.

"What's wrong?"

She tried to drop her gaze again, and he placed a firm finger under her chin to force her to look at him.

"This thing where you hide from me, it stops now. I can't fix things if you don't tell me what's going on."

His brain tried to make him consider why he felt so compelled to fix anything for a woman he barely knew. A woman who had deceived him. That was an internal battle for another day. Right now, he needed her to open to him.

"Was it like that with my sister too?"

He wanted to rage and ask her how she could possibly think that after the time they shared together. But again, there was that soft pleading in her eyes that was as effective as a gut punch in lowering his defenses and getting him to give her whatever she needed and wanted in that moment.

"Despite that fact that I believed you to be your sister, you are the only woman I've ever had such a visceral response to. My interactions with your sister have only ever been business-related. We've never had any personal conversations. Beyond what your company could do for my country's economy, I had zero interest in her."

He caressed her cheek, letting his thumb slide against the soft skin there while desire prickled at every inch of him.

"I need you to hear me and hear me well, Regina. This isn't an attempt to mock your sister or dismiss her beauty and presence in any way. But when I met with your sister earlier today, I couldn't figure out for the life of me why there was absolutely no attraction to her. Nothing about her remotely appealed to me. The only emotion she invoked was anger because I thought she was lying to me."

He took her hand, sliding it down his clothed form until her delicate fingers were cupping him through his pants.

"This is all for you. It was that night, and it is now."

The sadness in her retreated, and he had to wonder how long this had been plaguing her. Was she always in her sister's shadow? Was that why she didn't seem to think she compared with Reigna? Had some other man made her feel less than in comparison to her twin?

"I know it's childish. Especially considering I'm the one who let you think you were sleeping with my sister in the first place. But it mattered."

He nodded. "If it bothers you, if it upsets you, then it matters to me too. Is this what you and your sister were fighting about?"

Again, she tried to shift her gaze from his. "What did I say about hiding from me, Regina?"

Her eyes instantly snapped up to his, and the gift of her acquiescence burned through his veins like lava, scoring grooves into him and reshaping the landscape of his need.

"Yes. She thinks you might have some sort of twin kink and warned me away from you to protect me."

That might have been the gist of the conversation, yet everything in him believed that was the sanitized version of what Reigna had said.

Instinctively he knew that if Reigna had spoken those exact words, Regina wouldn't have been as hurt as she was. If he ever got the chance, he'd make the new queen know exactly what he thought about her reckless mouth when it came to her sister.

Not that he had any right to engage Reigna on Regina's behalf, but that was beside the point. He wouldn't allow anyone to push Regina into a shell of self-doubt again.

"Is this what it's going to be like if I agree to marry you and have your child? Are you always going to come to my rescue?"

"Whether you choose to marry me or not, have my child or not, I will always come when you need me."

The strength of his words comforted her and surprised him. He had no logical reason to make such assertions to her. But every instinct he had was to protect Regina. Even though she'd lied to him and that lie had put them all in a difficult position, it didn't matter. What mattered was when he saw need in her eyes, no matter whether it was sexual or emotional, he had the Pavlovian response to don his armor and protect her like the gallant kings of old.

CHAPTER SEVEN

REGINA SLOWLY CLIMBED out of the hold sleep had her in. She stretched, then remembered how she'd fallen asleep last night. She turned, hoping to find the king still lying beside her, but knowing somehow before her fingers found the cold sheets where he'd lain that he was gone.

A small ache that wasn't quite regret filled her chest as she thought about what had happened last night. He'd come to talk about his proposal. That was the only logical reason he'd shown up at her door. And yet when he'd seen her, he'd focused all his energy, all his words, on making her feel better.

She pulled herself up, swinging her legs out of the bed, and started her day with a quick shower. She threw on a pair of cream high-waisted slacks, a matching fitted crop top that fell just above her belt, and her favorite pair of Louboutins. A quick glance in the mirror at her size-sixteen form confirmed what she'd always known: fashionable and fabulous didn't have a dress size.

Intending to make a last stop in the kitchen for a cup of coffee before she headed to her lab, she ran into a solid wall of flesh. Before she could lose her balance, she felt a strong arm circle her waist, pulling her up against said wall.

She looked up to find amused blue eyes looking down at her with a matching grin to boot.

"Good morning, Treasure. How did you sleep?"

Being this close to him, she could smell the faint sweet and spicy tones of his cologne luring her to lean in and bury her nose in his chest. This chest had been pressed hard against her back as he cradled her while she slept.

Thinking over everything Aléx had said and done caused her to soften against him. Her sister had made him out to be a calculating monster. Considering he was a king, she was pretty sure that was a professional skill he had to expertly wield when necessary. The way he talked about duty and protecting his people, she was certain he didn't walk around pinching babies and kicking puppies all day either.

He was nothing like Reigna had made him out to be. How could he be when both times she was in his arms, he'd done everything to keep her safe and give her what she needed?

A spark of something warm and soothing

spread through her as she thought about how he cared for her. It almost reminded her of how looked-after Ace always made her feel.

Safe.

Secure.

Protected.

Wanted.

It was that last one that was doing something to her, that made her pull back and steady herself on her own two feet. When you grew up with toxic parents who didn't hide the fact that you were a nuisance, no matter how great your life became, there was always this inkling buried deep inside your cells that needed to be wanted.

"Since I didn't even notice you slip out of the bed, you know I slept well. What are you still doing here? I thought you would've been back on your throne making royal decrees and such."

The amusement in his eyes was contagious, making her lips draw into a full grin in response.

"You Americans really do have a fantastical imagination when it comes to what a working monarch actually does."

She lifted a shoulder before stepping around him and leaning against the counter in the middle of the room.

"All we've got to go on are Disney movies and *The Crown*. What do you expect?"

She made quick work of making a single-serve cup of coffee, but kept her eyes focused on the machine so she wouldn't have to be mesmerized by the sight of him.

"What I mean to say is that I can't imagine you have a whole lot of time for leisure. Why are you still here, letting me take up all your time?"

"I'm right where I want to be."

He was standing next to her in one stride, his more than six feet of solid, broad body making her look up at him in her stiletto heels.

"Do you feel better? Are you still upset by what your sister said to you?"

She gave herself a mental shake, not wanting to think about those dark parts of her that Reigna's words had hollowed out. Unknowingly triggering the internal murkiness she fought to keep at bay. Aléx's care had wiped the stains of those parts away, and she wanted them to remain locked out.

Regina had spent so much time playing understudy to Reigna's main character that she'd somehow become supporting cast in her own life too. As much as she wanted to blame her sister for her emotional mess, Regina couldn't. She'd allowed Reigna to take the lead because it made her sister feel secure. But now that Reigna was married and living in another country and Regina was left alone, she regretted not showing up more for herself in the past.

When she was with Aléx, she didn't feel invisible. He saw her. What she wouldn't give to feel seen like that always.

Isn't that what the king is offering you, a life where you're wanted, always? A life where you're seen?

As if on cue, he came to stand behind her, putting his strong hands on her shoulders and giving them a light squeeze.

"Are you all right?" His rich tenor wrapped around her, making her feel as cozy as his arms had the night before.

"I'm fine. It must have had something to do with the lavender bath and the human teddy bear I got to snuggle up with in my sleep."

"Excuse me, Treasure. I'll have you know that I am a big scary king, not a teddy bear."

There was little bite to his voice. He wasn't taking himself seriously at all, and somehow that made him all the more attractive to her.

"Thank you for what you did last night." She finally turned around and sought out his gaze. "I realize that I completely derailed the reason for your visit with my B.S."

His gaze fell on her hard, singed with heat, and not the good kind of heat either.

"According to my sister," he began, "I can present as cold at times." There was quiet again, and she realized there was some heft to not only what he'd said, but how he'd said it. His voice deep, yet reserved, as if he were trying to sift for the truth in his own words.

"I'm sure your sister knows you much better than I. By my measure, apart from when I told you who I really was, you've only ever been kind to me."

"Perhaps I should keep you around, since you think I'm so wonderful."

"Was that a not-so-subtle hint at your proposal?"

Her quip gifted her a deep rumble of laughter that made her smile even harder. Bringing him back to this playful side felt like the biggest accomplishment she'd ever achieved.

"Since you brought it up, have you given it more thought?"

Except for when she was telling him about her fight with her sister, she hadn't thought of anything else. It was ridiculous. It made no sense at all. The problem was, after the care he'd given her last night, she'd wanted more of it. Would he give her more if she said yes? Was that even a risk she could take?

"Regina." His words drew her out of her own head and lulled her into the wonderful warm place where she felt comfortable and safe. "Despite how short a time we've known each other, we make sense. You know it. You've felt it just like I have."

He ran a light hand down her arm, letting his fingers caress her flesh gently. Felt it? She'd done more than feel it. The connection between them had haunted her for four months with relentless repetition. In her lab, out shopping, on the subway, in a cab, thoughts of him and them had burned themselves on the walls of her mind, turning her every which way but loose.

The physical connection had been immediate and undeniable between them. Last night, however, had made her want more than the physical, and that was why this was so scary. She wanted more of him, more of them together, more of the feeling she had when he'd cared for her so intentionally.

"Aléx, I do feel our connection. I just don't know that it's enough to carry on a successful marriage. When I dreamed of marriage, I dreamed of love, of a man who would always put me first. I've literally spent my life playing second fiddle to someone else. What happens if we get married, and you finally find the love of your life? Do I become an afterthought? Will I be pushed aside to make way for her? Is my only purpose going to be to give you a child? What happens once I've fulfilled that?"

"Regina—"

"No," she interrupted him. "These are real

concerns, Aléx. I don't want to be stuck in a marriage where I'm invisible."

"You wouldn't be." He edged those words in, but she continued as if she hadn't heard him, because she needed to get all her worries out of her head.

"You've already told me that love won't be a factor. What assurances do I have that I won't just be the toy you pull out to show the rest of the world just how great you are and then behind the scenes, you barely interact with me? You not falling in sloppy love with me, I can handle. You pushing me to the periphery of your life and acting as if I don't matter, like I'm invisible and unimportant to you, I don't think I could live like that. I don't want my child growing up that way, believing people are disposable once they've fulfilled their designated purpose."

She tapped her acrylic nails against the white marble of the counter, hoping she didn't sound as desperate to him as she did to herself. He was probably regretting ever asking her at this point.

She was a strong and capable person. She didn't wallow in her feelings like this. Yet something inside her just couldn't let this go. Her insecurity about her position in people's lives had always been her Achilles' heel. It helped her discern how much effort and energy she gave to people. More importantly, it helped her decide how much of her heart to give.

"Regina." His voice had softened, smoothing out the rugged edges of her emotions. "As a king, I cannot be led by my emotions. As a man, love has seemed to do more harm than good. It's more often used as a weapon than a curative."

She couldn't rightly argue with him there. By all accounts, her parents were a love match. It was having children that destroyed their relationship. Perhaps if she approached it from the opposite way, maybe it might make for a better outcome.

She took a mental breath, berating herself.

This isn't an experiment. You can't science your way into a happy marriage, Regina.

"Love may not be part of our marriage, but care, concern, kindness, and consideration will be. I will take care of you every way I know how. There will never be another woman who comes before you. As my queen, it will be your right to expect that I put you first. As my wife, it will be my utter privilege to give you my devotion in mind, action and body. I promise you, Treasure, you will never doubt where you stand with me."

Her heart thumped harder in her chest. For a man who didn't believe in love, his words certainly painted the opposite picture. Because to her, everything he said made her want to fall hard for him.

"The only thing I need to know is," he continued, "...are you willing to offer me the same?"

This man and his charming and tender words were going to be the end of her. She absolutely knew it. How could she not want to run straight off the proverbial cliff just for a chance at a taste of what he was offering? She might never have been in love, but everything he offered her sounded like heaven to her weary soul.

"This marriage will be real, Regina. Whether or not you decide to continue our physical relationship beyond conception is immaterial. Our bond and our fate will be sealed. This is forever. Can you handle that?"

She was primed to agree, even though the tiny voice in her head kept asking her if she'd be able to live without love. Would it be so bad? Would she miss what she'd never had? No man had connected with her in a way that made her think a future was possible...before now. And then it suddenly occurred to her, there was something else they hadn't discussed that she had to get straight before she signed up for this.

"I can," she murmured, her mind still pulling out her metaphorical shield to protect her if what she said next made this conversation go left.

"Are we agreed, then?" His voice had so much

hope that it was beginning to stir her own. But first, they had to get this all hammered out.

"No, we're not. Not yet. Aléx?"

"Yes, Treasure?"

Every time he used that pet name, some of the cold iciness she often tried to guard the delicate parts of her with melted a little more. But she couldn't get lost in how this man was making her feel. She had to ask the tough questions.

"I'm a Black woman."

"I'm aware." His answer was matter-of-fact, like race didn't matter.

She took a deep breath and pressed forward. "How are your people, your court, your family and friends going to react to you making me your queen? I've seen how Europeans like to tussle about their monarchies. I'm not trying to end up in a situation where I'm running from Obsidian Island with my children in tow because folks can't accept a Black woman as their queen."

When he was quiet and the silence stretched long beyond her patience, she spoke again.

"And if you tell me you don't see color, I'll twist your lips into a knot."

He chuckled, which was slightly comforting. If she'd seen disdain, disinterest or cluelessness in his eyes, her fight-or-flight response would have been humming in the background. Instead, she'd be out the door and getting into her car instead of standing here waiting on his next words.

She'd moved in corporate America for a good portion of her life. In those rarified circles, white people often tried to pretend they lived in a post-racial world. Her experience as a curvy Black woman from Brooklyn said otherwise. She couldn't go into this blind without knowing what she was facing.

"Obsidian Island isn't in Europe. It's in North America. We lie somewhere in the middle between Nova Scotia in Canada and Bermuda."

She rolled her eyes at his geography lesson. "Sir, you have a Greek name and look like John Stamos is your daddy. Are you really trying to argue that you don't have some European blood in your veins?"

She folded her arms, waiting for an answer, because they both knew she was right. "I wouldn't try to argue your point," he responded. "I couldn't. My mother was a direct descendant of the deposed royalty in Greece."

She went to turn away from him, and Aléx wrapped gentle fingers around her wrist, stroking the soft skin there in a silent plea for her to stay.

"I would never ignore your concerns regarding this matter. Race is very much still an issue, even on a small island nation like Obsidian Island. What I will tell you is that I will not tolerate any disrespect, outright or otherwise, at your expense. Not that this should allay your fears, but you won't be the first Black queen or monarch on the throne."

That made her cock an eyebrow, positive that the disbelief on her face was as visible as a neon sign. He was right that history didn't mean things would be a bed of roses. It simply meant she wouldn't be the first. Being the first in these situations always sucked.

"Really?" she asked.

She pulled out a chair at her eat-in counter, and he took the one immediately next to her, crowding her space and her senses.

"Yes, really," he replied in earnest. "I'll have to show you the Hall of Kings and Queens when you come back with me."

She hadn't missed that *when* in the sentence either. Listening to him, she couldn't decide if it was confidence or conceit that had him believing her leaving with him was an inevitability.

"We share the same land mass with Nyeusi, much like Haiti and the Dominican Republic. Since a good bit of the land that connects us is submerged below sea level, this makes travel between the two nations by boat and helicopter relatively easy. Now that we've built a bridge, traveling by car is possible too." He brought her back to the conversation. "Our peoples, including royals, have migrated back and forth as well as married throughout the centuries. Of course that doesn't magically make race relations better."

She couldn't call what his candidness made her feel relief. More like appreciation that he'd heard her concerns and hadn't tried to gaslight her into believing this wasn't an issue she should be bringing up. Glad to have that over with, she tried to bring some levity into the situation.

"Wow, King Aléxandros. It almost sounds like you're signing on to be my hero, defending my honor like you've described. Does that mean you'd send people to the dungeons for me, wage war for me?"

"No." His voice was sharp and clear as he placed a finger under her chin, making her gaze fasten onto his. "It means I'd raze the ground they stood on for you. I'm not attempting to be your hero, Regina. Heroes don't exist. I'm trying to be your husband. I'm trying to show you that you'll never have to fight alone ever again."

That startled her. The idea of getting to lay down her weapons because someone else would protect her affected her on a level so deep, she could feel its impact running through her blood and bone. Black women in America didn't get to rest. They had to be three times better than anyone else to get marginally ahead. They were expected to be the mules of society, carrying all its burdens and nurturing everyone else except their families and loved ones. What he was offering her...felt like a balm to her soul.

Discomfort twisted in the bottom of her belly as reality screamed at her with a metaphorical bullhorn to make sure she heard it. She did, and recognized it for what it was, doubt. She still doubted him. Not that she believed he was lying, because his conviction came through in the steel of his voice. It was that history, both her personal history and the history of her people, that taught her to make people show and prove when it came to garnering her trust.

"Regina." He whispered her name, letting the sound pin her right where she sat. "Ultimately it comes down to this: Do you think you can trust me? If you can, I believe we can give each other everything we want."

Hearing his words was like being submerged in an ice river during a blizzard, shocking her system.

"Aléx, we're not each getting everything we want."

"All right then, what else is missing?"

Love, that's what's missing. Love.

The words were on the tip of her tongue, but she couldn't bring herself to say them. After Ace had rescued her and her sister from their terrible parents, she'd promised herself she'd never beg for love again, never believe blindly. And she never would.

"You're asking for marriage and a child, and devoted companionship. I need something more than that."

There wasn't a single second of hesitation in his voice. "Name it and it's yours."

"I need you to provide the seed capital and a fully stocked and staffed laboratory so I can create the Black hair care line I want to start."

This wasn't about being mercenary or transactional. This was about him taking on as much risk as her. In her estimation, the phrase "put your money where your mouth is" was an unassailable truth. If this all went to hell, at least she knew she'd walk away with something, even if she wound up losing her heart.

She didn't need his money or resources for this. She could pull the funds from her own accounts. She could find investors right here in the States. Her family owned a venture capital company, for goodness' sake. The money was literally at her fingertips. But if she chose any of those options, her sister would know. And if Reigna knew, she'd find a way to name all the logical reasons Regina was making a bad decision. Damn her logical brain. Regina's penchant for reason over emotion would force her to give in to her sister.

That could not happen again. Regina needed this. If she couldn't have the love she wanted, perhaps the child and the business of her heart would more than make up for it.

"Agreed," Aléx replied. "Now I just need to know when you want to get married."

"How soon can you get us back to Obsidian Island?"

And just like that, they were entering into an agreement to get married and have a kid. Panic should have been assailing her, should have had her clawing at her own throat to get air. Strangely, there was no panic, only rightness. Which meant one of two things. She was either in need of a mental competency exam, or maybe, just maybe, her instincts were forcing her to do what her mind and heart could never conceive of. Maybe, with Aléx's help, she could actually reach for her dreams and step out of her sister's shadow.

CHAPTER EIGHT

ALÉX TAPPED HIS finger against the arm of the plush leather chair of his plane. He looked around the large cabin, trying to distract himself, trying to pretend he wasn't worried that Regina would come to her senses and realize she could do so much better than a man who could never love her.

Love had gutted him, carved a cavernous hole in his chest that left him unable to hold something so precious. He'd tried it. Had given it everything he had, and when life cruelly snatched it away, he'd barely been able to survive. Thank God his father was still around then to fill in the gaps as his regent, and his sister had taken on as many of Aléx's duties as she could. Together they had borne the weight of the crown when he could hardly find a reason to get out of bed, to breathe, to live.

His chest tightened with long-buried memories that tried to climb out of the pit he'd thrown them in, making him physically shudder as he beat them back into the darkness. He would not go back there. He couldn't. Not again, not ever. He could never be that weak, broken and useless again.

"Your Majesty."

The sound of his personal secretary's voice using his courtesy title pulled him from his morose thoughts and forced him to step into the role he was literally born to play. King Aléxandros of Obsidian Island. That man was strong and could endure anything.

"Ms. Devereaux's car is pulling up to the tarmac," Michael continued. "Would you like me to have her brought directly on board when she arrives?"

If she were anyone else, he would have been more than fine with that. The problem was, Regina never was anyone else. Even when he thought she was her sister, she was so different from anyone else he'd ever met, including the actual Reigna Devereaux.

"No, I'll bring her on myself."

He stood to his full height, squaring his shoulders and straightening his spine. His strides were long, eating up the path through the cabin, down the steps and to the tarmac. He arrived in time to see his security team opening the back door of the black limousine he'd sent for her.

Forever the charming king, he offered her a

waiting hand and was gifted with a wide grin that lit up her face. It rocked him, forcing him to plant his feet so that they both didn't tip over when she placed a foot outside the car and stood on the skinniest pair of red stilettos he'd ever seen. Those shoes made electricity thrum through him, making him want to forget they stood in the open for all to see.

The sound of staffers pulling her luggage out of the car made him keep a tight leash on the desire her mere presence was stoking in him. It was a damn inconvenient time for his body to wrestle against his control.

He took a breath before taking in the full view of her. Regina was a beautiful woman in any circumstance. She'd been breathtaking in that cocktail dress when he'd met her. Today she was stunning in a fitted silk tee with cap sleeves paired with black high-waisted tailored pants that stopped just under her bust. She had business casual down to a science, and instead of making him want to crunch numbers, it made him want to peel every stitch of clothing she wore away from what he knew was the plush body of a voluptuous goddess with the softest skin he'd ever touched.

"Your Majesty." She greeted him with a teasing smirk that toyed with his self-control the way sweet cakes and candy tempted the most mischievous child. She was daring him to reprimand her about her calling him by his title.

It grated on everything inside him to hear her call him anything but what he called himself in his head. Aléxandros was the king. Aléx was the man. And more than anything, he wanted—no, needed—this woman to see him as a man. The king was what he did. The man was who he was.

"I hope Obsidian Island is ready for me, because Brooklyn is about to be in the house."

He placed her hand in the curve of his bent arm and leaned down to place a chaste kiss on her cheek.

"I don't think anyone on Obsidian Island is ready for you, Regina, least of all me. But I somehow think we'll all be the better for being graced by your presence."

Again, she blessed him with that big, beautiful smile, and all he wanted to do was tug her into his side and give her reason after reason to keep smiling at him with the same exuberance she was nearly blinding him with right now.

He remembered the last time he'd been this affected by a smile. Memories of a tall, slender woman with sandy brown hair and curious brown eyes looking back at him assailed him. The image was so sharp and so clear, he had to clutch the armrest to keep from reaching for her. As soon as the image came, it was gone, snatched away from him like she had been in real life.

Pain and regret traveled like bile from his gut, burning its way up his throat. When would his suffering stop? When would he be rid of this regret and guilt that always reminded him he wasn't worthy of love?

"Aléx, are you okay?"

He blinked away his thoughts and, through sheer muscle memory, used all his public speaking training to turn on his kingly charm and assuage the worry he saw building in Regina's pinched expression.

"I'm fine, Treasure. I'm simply cataloging the things I need to set in motion once we touch down."

She turned her head to get a glance around the cabin. "I'm sure this plush plane has Wi-Fi capabilities. You don't have to entertain me."

He pulled her hand into his and pressed his lips to the tops of her fingers. Her hands were soft and warm, inviting him to take the peace she unknowingly offered him. He'd felt it the night they'd met. He'd felt safe and cared for, and worthy in her presence. The last four months without her had left him short-tempered with chaos knocking around inside him.

All that rage and noise quieted once he'd learned the woman who'd had such an impact on him that neither his body nor his mind could forget her wasn't married to another king. He could have this again; all he had to do was keep her happy and show her his world wasn't something to fear, and he would protect her from any and all threats.

"I couldn't be better, Treasure. I'm just anxious to get you back home and make you my queen. The future we will have will be brilliant. You'll never want to leave."

"I think you're right. I don't ever want to leave this place."

Regina stood slack-jawed as she took in the ocean view from the balcony in his private chamber. He'd purposely chosen this side of the palace so he'd wake up to seeing the sun kissing the sea, and the water making the island's black sand sparkle like a flawless onyx.

"I've never seen black sand before."

The glimmer of excitement in her eyes made him proud. Obsidian Island was part of him, after all. Knowing that she saw the same beauty in his homeland made his chest fill with pride.

"It's very rare." He pointed out the coastline. "That's certainly part of its charm."

"I'm sure there's so many more charming things about it than the sand. Tell me about its history."

He closed his hand around hers, gently directing her away from the balcony, through his quarters and downstairs. Regina could hardly keep up as she took in their surroundings. Impossibly high ceilings, Roman pillars, and antique furniture and fabrics that were as old as the nation itself grabbed her interest with ease. She hardly noticed they'd arrived at their destination until he released her hand and opened the set of thirty-foot double doors that partitioned the room off from the rest of the palace.

"This is the Hall of Kings and Queens. It's the place where we honor the rulers of old, paying homage to their lives and their legacies."

They stopped by a large glass statue of a woman dressed in regal attire with her scepter clutched tightly between her hands.

"She is breathtaking. Who is she?"

He could feel the sad smile curving his lips. "Queen Carisse. She was my mother. Her reign lasted thirty years. She died eight years ago."

"And your father?"

"Six years later." He cleared his throat, trying to keep the dull ache of loss at bay. He'd adored both his parents, and being without them still made him feel unbalanced, like he wasn't quite himself.

"He, my sister, Eliana and I had our weekly family dinner. We reminisced about old times when it was still the four of us. He was happy, but tired, so he went to bed and went silently in his sleep."

"I'm so sorry, Aléx. I can see you still feel their loss."

"She was loud and boisterous and took up so much space in the room and life, and he was quiet and insightful. Together they were an unstoppable pair. It would be impossible not to feel their loss. They were amazing parents. But as monarch and consort, there aren't very many who can match their greatness. They passed on an incredible legacy to me and my sister."

She peered up at him, carefully assessing him as she spoke. "This legacy thing really is important to you, isn't it? You wanting an heir isn't just an act of ego?"

He leaned down and ran his finger over the gold plate at the base of his mother's statue. Sometimes, if he stared long enough at the statue at just the right angle, he swore he could almost see her form overlaid over the mold.

"Make no mistake, I do want a child. My desire aside, however, it really is my job. Securing the monarchy isn't just about wanting to enjoy royal trappings. We come from a line of people who have dedicated their lives in service to this land and its people. Fulfilling all those duties in the best way I can is my sole focus as king."

"Your people are lucky to have you."

"No, I'm lucky to serve them."

He took her hand and moved her further into the room, stopping to share interesting facts about his home and its history until they stopped in front of a large oil painting of a man with the same Mediterranean features Aléx bore and a darker-skinned woman with a large, tightly coiled Afro that stood as proud as the crown on her head.

"This is King Nikos. He was my fourth great-grandfather. The beautiful woman beside him is my fourth great-grandmother, Queen Nairobi, princess of Nyeusi, third daughter of King Amir of the House of Adebesi."

He could see her doing the calculations in her head, watching the intense concentration on her face as her mind took in all the factors and came to the inevitable conclusion.

"You and Jasiri share an ancestor?"

"We share three, in fact." When she opened her mouth to speak, he held up his hand. "All in different generations and different centuries. Queen Nairobi is our closest shared relative."

"Was your family here when Nyeusi was formed? Were your people part of The Trade?"

A chill ran down his spine as she stared directly at him, silently demanding his answer.

By her use of "The Trade," he knew she was

referring to the Transatlantic Slave Trade. Nyeusi had become a nation when enslaved people from the 1741 New York Slave Conspiracy were wrongfully accused of sabotaging military bases and were sentenced to enslavement in the Caribbean or death in the colonies. Those brave souls overpowered their captors and were saved when they found themselves on an uninhabited island where they could live out the rest of their lives free.

"No, we weren't." His voice rang out strong in the room, echoing off the various monuments to his ancestors as if they were answering with him in unison.

"Some of those men who'd attempted to enslave Nyeusi's ancestors washed up on our shores. Our people took them in, unaware of who they were. We offered them food and shelter until Obsidians realized they were slavers. When they finally revealed themselves to be in search of an alliance in their unholy cause, we took them back to Nyeusi and turned them over for justice at the hands of those they'd wronged. From that moment, Obsidian Island and Nyeusi have been allies. We still are, even if I think their king is an arrogant tool."

"Hey, that's your cousin and my brother-in-law. Don't talk about him like that."

"He is my very distant cousin, this is true. We

grew up together. Our parents were very close, and we were too."

"Were? Are you not close now?"

Aléx stepped closer to the painting of Queen Nairobi. With her uncompromising beauty and countenance, she made a fierce queen. Although they shared no blood, he could see the same qualities in Regina.

Refocusing on her question, he answered her. "Jasiri was raised very differently from me. His parents encouraged him going out into the world and experiencing life as a man and not an heir to a throne. It made him a bit wild and careless at times. I was raised to only focus on duty, to forget the self. Carelessness isn't something I easily give in to."

He wanted so badly to finish that sentence, to tell her of the one time he had been careless, and the consequences that unfolded as a result. Consequences he was still paying for to this day with a piece of his soul. Instead, he took the coward's way out and let quietness fill the room as thoughts of Jasiri filled his mind.

They had been fast friends as children. Jasiri had always brought a lightheartedness to Aléx's world he'd missed dearly when they began to grow apart.

You mean, when you distanced yourself from him, right?

That was the truth. He had pulled away once he'd learned that Jasiri would be allowed to live in America as a Nyeusian ambassador after he'd completed university. When Aléx had finished university, he'd been summoned home to take on more royal responsibilities so that when he ascended to the throne, he would already be familiar with the process and the protocol of ruling.

Instead of being man enough to own his jealousy, he'd removed himself from Jasiri's life until the two men rarely spoke. Aléx isolated himself until he was left with nothing but his work and his immediate family.

That same sort of pettiness had cost him everything that mattered to him. When his ex, Farah, had left him, he'd slowly pulled away from her too. If he'd just had the courage to step outside her rejection of him, things might have worked out very differently, and he wouldn't have a blood debt marking his soul.

He would not make that same mistake with Regina. He would keep her close no matter what.

She slid her hand into his palm, and he sheltered it there. More and more he was finding he always wanted to shelter her. When he'd found her upset in her apartment, something ugly and possessive had churned inside him. His automatic response was to make sure she was okay and protect her from anyone who would dare hurt her, including her twin sister.

He'd question himself later about why that was. In this moment, like last night, he just wanted her to feel cared for, supported. From what little he'd gleaned about her relationship with her sister, he got the distinct impression that Regina's needs and wants were never brought to the center.

"Thank you for sharing that with me. It's an interesting bit of history I would never have garnered anywhere else in the world."

"Not even Nyeusi?" He knew that Nyeusi was rich with cultural reverence for the blood they'd shed to ensure their freedom.

"I've not really spent much time on Nyeusi. My sister's been married for less than six months. They're still in the honeymoon phase. The last thing they need is me underfoot."

He looked down at her, squeezing her hand to get her to meet his eye. "Do you always do that?" When she narrowed her gaze to silently ask him what he meant, he continued, "Do you always shrink yourself for your sister? Is that what she demands of you?"

Fire flashed in her eyes as she stared at him with sharp intention. "My sister loves me. You've known me for two days, basically. You don't get to pass judgment on her or me."

"You can deflect all you want, Treasure." He held her attention with his steadfast gaze. "I'm not going to let this drop. Does Reigna demand this kind of allegiance from you?"

He cupped her chin, forcing her to keep her eyes on him. He was learning that Regina was a fighter, and she would more than likely keep fighting if she thought it would get her out of explaining.

"I'm not going anywhere, Treasure. Tell me the truth."

The fight in her eyes retreated. She was slowly letting down her guard for him. It was a gift he would always handle with reverence.

"I don't want you to think Reigna is purposely malicious to me. She's not. My sister loves me, and I love her. In her head, I'm the little sister she needs to take care of, fuss over and protect. She doesn't want me to be small. She just doesn't want me to grow. Growing would mean I wouldn't need her."

"And you let her believe you do?" Although it was phrased as a question, he very much meant it as a statement.

"Yes," she replied as she stepped away from him, walking through the room and stopping to take in each display. This was classic avoidance behavior. But he wasn't about to let her get away with it.

When she was a few paces away from him, as if his proximity somehow made it hard to shape her thoughts, she said, "It's my way of taking care of her."

Understanding dawned. She wasn't weak. She simply allowed her sister to believe that.

He laid gentle hands on her shoulders and leaned down with his lips touching the shell of her ear. It was intimate, her scent almost intoxicating. But this wasn't about physicality. This was about his uncontrollable need to care for the woman who'd cared for him.

"Be careful, Treasure. If you keep shrinking yourself, eventually you'll disappear. And that will just never do. You will be a queen in two days. The queens of Obsidian Island are just as fierce as its kings, if not more so. Court is not for the faint of heart. You'll have to show them you can't be run over."

He saw the defiant spark in her eyes slightly letting loose the woman who had given and received pleasure like she was made explicitly for him. That was the woman he wanted to rule at his side. That was the woman who would be the mother of his children.

"I'm not worried, Treasure. I know you've got some teeth to you. I've felt them at work."

CHAPTER NINE

REGINA'S HEAD WAS SPINNING. She rested in her bed, trying to catch her breath while she could, because tomorrow was the day. Tomorrow, she would marry Aléx and become queen of Obsidian Island. How was this even her life?

Aléx had asked her if she wanted the big fancy wedding every queen was supposed to crave. She'd declined immediately. It seemed out of place when she knew she wasn't getting the whole deal. Those kinds of weddings were for people who were sloppy in love. That was not who she and Aléx were.

To expedite matters, she'd opted for a small ceremony in Aléx's drawing room with just them and Aléx's sister, Eliana. He'd informed her that they would eventually have a large observance that included her official coronation. For now, however, he would give her the small occasion, allowing her time to adjust to royal life before he presented her officially to the world.

An ache settled in her heart as she thought

of both of Reigna's weddings. In both the civil and formal ceremonies, Regina had been right by Reigna's side. Despite the hurt her sister had heaped on her, Regina still wanted her here. Still wanted her support. Still wanted her love.

Her cell phone rang at that exact moment, and she didn't even have to look at the screen to know who it was. Regina didn't know if it was because they were twins or because they were just so close that they always seemed to sense when the other needed them.

Regina grabbed the phone, accepted the call and put the phone to her ear.

"What's wrong with my sister?"

That question, formed in her sister's sultry voice, was almost her undoing. It was the question they'd asked each other from the time since they'd learned to talk whenever they knew the other was hurting.

Before Regina could answer, Reigna spoke again. "Regina, I'm sorry that I hurt you. I was out of line, and I didn't mean any of it. I've tried to give you space to process. But no one in the office has seen you in two days, and I'm afraid something has happened to you. Please tell me what's going on."

Quiet tears streamed down Regina's cheeks. Keeping this secret from her sister was tying her in knots.

Her decision to keep what she and Aléx were planning a secret was selfish on so many levels. She'd done it partly to spite Reigna. Mostly, though, it was because she knew if she told Reigna the truth, her sister would go into protective mode. Regina would have to deal with Reigna's emotions instead of figuring out if Aléx's offer was the right thing for her.

"I'm fine, Reigna. I promise. I haven't been in the office because I've been spending some time with Aléx on Obsidian Island."

She heard Reigna's intake of breath and started speaking again before Reigna could interrupt.

"And if you start up again about Aléx not wanting me, I promise I will hang up and turn my phone off."

"You really like this man, don't you?"

If it were only as simple as liking him. She wouldn't go as far as to say she was in love with Aléx, but there was this underlying connection between them that she couldn't easily walk away from.

"I do."

"You sure he's dealt with the mistaken identity thing? Being queen means I have a plane at my disposal. I can be over there before you can say, 'Your Majesty.'"

Regina couldn't help the bubble of laughter climbing up her throat.

"I know you can. But I promise, everything with Aléx is going great."

"Okay?" Her sister's inquisitive but playful tone traveled through the line as clearly as if she were seated right beside Regina. "Tell me how good?"

Regina swallowed the lump in her throat, hoping she didn't end up regretting this. She knew even if she did, she loved her sister. She just wasn't built to lie to her no matter how much she didn't want to deal with her big-sister bullshit.

"If I tell you this, you have to promise me that you trust me, and you know I wouldn't do anything stupid."

"Regina." Reigna's skeptical huff made Regina smile.

"Promise. I really need my sister right now, and it sucks that I can't share some really incredible news with you because you think I'm naive when it comes to people."

The line was quiet. Regina could envision her sister biting her tongue until it bled to keep from antagonizing the younger twin.

"Regina, I won't lie to you. I do think you're naive when it comes to interpersonal interactions with people. Staying locked up in your lab all the time, you just haven't had as much practice. But you're the smartest person I know, and I do trust you. I just worry about you so much. You're my little sister, and if someone is messing with you, they gotta fight me first."

The image of her sister squared up in her royal regalia with her baby bump poking out made her howl with laughter.

"Chile, you are four months pregnant. The only thing you fighting right now is buttoned jeans."

Reigna reciprocated with an equally loud howl of laughter before she said, "Girl, you ain't ever lied. If it ain't elastic, I ain't wearing it. I'm over here giving the royal seamstress a fit because she's had to modify all my fancy clothes with elastic waists. Apparently, *elastic* is like a curse word in the palace."

Their laughter quieted before Reigna began to speak again. "Stop stalling. Tell me this good news. I promise, whatever it is, I'll be supportive if it means as much to you as it seems to."

There was the sister she loved. The sister who had always been there for her through all the rough times they'd suffered when they lived with their parents. This was the sister she could share everything with.

"Tomorrow... Aléx and I are getting married. You're not going to be the only queen in the family."

Regina waited for her sister to blow her top, to start yelling and telling her she didn't have the sense God gave a goat. It wasn't like she hadn't been saying the same thing to herself since she'd agreed to Aléx's proposal.

"He came to see me the morning after you and I fought," Reigna said.

That got Regina's attention.

"He did? What did he want?"

Reigna was quiet again, as if she were contemplating how to convey her next thought. Reigna wasn't necessarily known for her calm. If you angered her, she would pop off in an instant. But as CEO of Gemini Queens, she'd learned to temper her anger when she needed to. Considering Reigna had gone radio silent after their fight, she knew her sister was doing everything in her power to curb her tongue. Regina couldn't love Reigna more for that in this moment.

"Ostensibly," Reigna began, "he came to apologize to me for accusing me of hiding his child from him."

The hair at the back of Regina's neck prickled, waiting for Reigna to drop the proverbial other shoe.

"He was sincere in his apology, but he also came for another reason."

"For goodness' sake, Reigna, spit it out. What did he want?"

Reigna chuckled at Regina's impatience. Usually, it was Reigna who was snapping at Regina to get to the point. This was just more proof that this man was changing things in her life, possibly even changing her.

"He came to tell me to back off where you're concerned. He told me you were upset, and you felt like I didn't believe in you. He told me that my meddling made you doubt yourself, and he demanded I mind how I spoke to you and stay out of your relationship with him, because he wasn't going anywhere."

Panic settled in her bones. Those were fighting words if she'd ever heard them. Regina took a breath, letting calm spread throughout her being. Since Aléx was still in possession of all his faculties and his limbs, Regina was certain this heart-to-heart couldn't have gone too terribly. Again, Reigna was the firecracker in the family. That was especially true when she was angry. And Reigna being told about herself where her twin sister was concerned was a surefire way to piss that woman off.

"Considering he's still walking under his own power, I'm assuming you didn't try to commit regicide at this meeting." That got Regina a loud bark of laughter that broke the tension.

"Oh, I contemplated it." Reigna's huff was halfway between serious and "girl, you know I'm just teasing." "I told him I don't play about my sister. I also told him if he hurt you, he wouldn't have to worry about Jasiri's wrath. His pales in comparison when it comes to how I protect who and what's mine."

"Is that all you said?" Regina knew her sister, and this recitation of what had to be a heated exchange between Aléx and Reigna was all too polite as far as Regina was concerned.

"I told him, when it came to him hurting my sister, and I quote, 'Please don't fuck around and find out… Your Majesty.'"

Regina howled. Not that she condoned threatening people. However, since she'd made a similar threat to Jasiri regarding Reigna, Regina didn't exactly have room to throw stones.

"If I told you that I wasn't mad at what he dared to say to me, I'd be lying," Reigna continued. "But it needed to be said. I hadn't taken the time to really see that I was undermining you and not protecting you. For that, I'm rightly convicted and so terribly sorry. I owed you better, and your king made me see that."

Regina marveled at the turn of the conversation. She'd expected this chat to have gone in an entirely different direction. But this was Aléx changing everything for her with great ease, apparently.

"Regina, if he was willing to fight me over a woman he'd just reconnected with after four months of no contact, he must really care about you. As much as I didn't like his tone, I couldn't be mad at him for protecting my sister better than I ever had. And please understand," Reigna added quickly, "that is the only reason I didn't lose my ever-loving mind and snap his neck."

The line went quiet again as Regina processed everything her sister had said. What Aléx had done was brave, exceptionally ill-advised, but still brave nonetheless. Apparently, he'd truly meant it when he'd said he would put her first in all things.

"Are you happy, sister?"

Regina thought about Reigna's question, and deep down, she knew the answer. Even if it didn't make a lick of logical sense.

"Yes, sister, I am."

"Then that's all that matters to me. I want to be there. I want to stand up for you the way you stood up for me. Will you let me?"

Her eyes watered, and her heart swelled. Her sister was coming through for her, and damn if it didn't have Regina all weepy and emotional. She was the logical twin, damn it. Why couldn't she keep her eyes dry in her interactions with her sister as of late?

I wonder if sympathetic pregnancy emotions are a thing in twins? This had to be because of Reigna's pregnancy. It couldn't possibly have anything to do with her.

She'd have to look that up later and see if there was any science behind it. But right now, the only thing she managed was saying, "I wouldn't have it any other way."

The ceremony had been quick and quiet, and now their very small gathering of close family was moving about, enjoying wedding cake and champagne. Regina was utterly alluring in her white two-piece pantsuit accented by a matching corset. Her curves were on display, and he wanted to peel that suit off her, but these people were still in the room, extinguishing any hope he had of consummating his marriage in this moment.

"I recognize that look."

Aléx looked to his side to see Jasiri, his distant cousin and the current king of Nyeusi.

"And what look is that, Your Majesty?"

Jasiri leaned his broad body against the wall where Aléx stood, jostling him with an elbow nudge.

"The look that says you want everyone out because you can't take your eyes off your bride."

Jasiri wasn't wrong. He rarely was. That was probably the most annoying thing about the man. That and his effortless carefree air that always made Aléx want to shake him.

"You would know. From the rumors, you

didn't leave Reigna's side through all three of your receptions or your coronation on your wedding day."

Jasiri nodded as he placed a forkful of cake in his mouth. "Exactly. And while you have that same hunger in your eyes, I have to wonder why you aren't plastered against your wife. I smell a marriage of convenience."

Aléx's entire body stiffened at Jasiri's words. Aléx wasn't ashamed of why he'd married Regina. But he wouldn't have anyone taking a cheap shot at her. Not even his royal cousin.

"This coming from the man who married his ex-girlfriend to be eligible to ascend to the throne. I don't think you have any room to throw stones."

Jasiri set his plate down, drawing himself up so that his back was to the room as he spoke so no one else could hear.

"I adore my wife, and by extension, my sister-in-love."

"Sister-in-love?"

Jasiri's exasperated sigh made Aléx want to smile. Good. He wasn't the only one annoyed with this conversation, then.

"It's how Reigna refers to in-laws. She says it's not the law that makes them family, but love. I love her sister," Jasiri continued. "I'm as protective of her as I am of my wife. Don't screw her over, Aléxandros, or you'll have to deal with me. Everyone knows you're not over—"

Aléx held up his hand, silencing Jasiri immediately. "Finish that sentence and you might not make it back to your throne in one piece... *cousin*."

The two men stared at each other. Both large with broad bodies, capable of matching each other's strength and rage.

"What happened to you, Aléx, was unthinkable. Nevertheless, I don't want Regina to live in someone else's shadow. Does she even know what happened?"

Aléx dipped his head, feeling the weight of his shame hit him. "No, she doesn't."

Jasiri clapped a hand on Aléx's shoulder. It was firm...yet it was supportive, as if he were really concerned for his cousin four or five times removed.

"Take it from someone whose secrets nearly cost him the love of an incredible woman. Don't hide your past from her. Let her help you with it. Because if you hurt her, Reigna will cut your balls off. And after she's done, you'll have to deal with me."

Jasiri's threat about Reigna made him shiver. He'd seen what a cutthroat businesswoman she was. After their tense conversation about her treatment of Regina, he'd had no doubt she'd slice him into tiny pieces if he hurt her sister. Neither of them had anything to worry about. Love might not be the basis of their marriage, but care and concern were.

"I'd rather cut off my own arm before I hurt her. She's special to me, Jasiri."

"Because she bears the same face as her sister?"

Anger simmered beneath Aléx's cool facade. The insinuation pissed him off, quite frankly. However, considering how their connection began, he couldn't rightly blame Jasiri either.

"I might not have known her real name when I met her, but trust me, she's the only sister I wanted then or now. Let's leave it at that before either of us says something we regret."

"Good," Jasiri said as a pleased smile set across his lips.

He was just about to step away when Aléx called after him.

"Jasiri, let that be the last time you insinuate my wife plays second to your wife, or any other woman, for that matter. If you do it again, I'll consider that an act of war and govern myself accordingly."

Jasiri's smile widened even further, showing every one of his perfect teeth. "That's exactly what a king and husband should do when someone insults his wife. You scorch the goddamn earth to protect her and her dignity at all costs. As long as you do that for Regina, you'll never hear a word from me."

The twins caught sight of the two of them and made their way to each of them respectively. Regina slid into Aléx's embrace instinctively as he pulled her into his side. This was where she belonged. It didn't matter that they weren't in love or hadn't come together in the traditional sense. She was his wife, and as he'd told Jasiri, he'd never let anyone hurt her.

Are you including yourself in that?

He closed his eyes and breathed in her sweet scent, trying to ignore the voice in his head. He could do this. He could protect and care for someone again. He would do it, no matter how much his fear tried to tell him otherwise.

"Are you ready to retire, Treasure?"

She looked up at him with queries in her eyes, questions she wanted to ask. But the soft kiss he placed on her lips prevented her from verbalizing them.

Tonight would be about them and not the ghosts of his past. If only for tonight, he would be free of his pain and give everything he had to Queen Regina. The woman who had quite literally turned his world upside down.

CHAPTER TEN

REGINA STOOD ON the balcony of the cottage they'd be spending their wedding night in. According to Aléx, this was the place where every Obsidian monarch spent their first night with their spouse. She'd tried to tell him they didn't have to bother, but he'd insisted. She was his queen, and she would be treated as such.

Regina tried to settle the dull ache in her chest as she thought about the situation she'd willingly put herself in. She had no right to be sad. This marriage was a business deal, not a love affair. Of course she would spend her wedding night alone. It wasn't a real wedding, and this wasn't a real marriage.

Outside the legality of it all, she and Aléx, for all intents and purposes, were roommates and business partners.

You agreed to that. No need to be upset about it now.

To lift her mood, she'd put on a silk robe and

camisole set that stopped at the middle of her thick thighs. Regina loved the way lingerie felt against her skin. It was silky, caressing her softly, and putting her curves on display at the same time. Every night, whether she slept alone or not, she put something soft and silky on her skin to love on herself.

Tonight, she needed to love on herself more than she ever had.

Standing on the balcony and watching the waves ebb and flow slowly against the rocks calmed the fears trying to claw their way through her system. She looked down at the square diamond sitting on a bed of small round white diamonds and the infinity diamond ring Aléx had placed on her finger today.

Her body warmed with his thoughtfulness and generosity. She hadn't expected something like this, marveling at it as the moonlight twinkled in its facets. She'd told him it was too much, and he'd replied that it wasn't enough.

This man was so sweet to her it was killing her. How was she not supposed to fall for him when he did and said sweet things like that?

I don't know how you're gonna manage, but you bet'not fall for that man. He doesn't want love, remember? He only wants a baby and companionship.

Before she could ruminate harder on her intrusive thoughts, a knock at the bedroom door drew her attention.

Aléx walked in wearing nothing but his silk pajama bottoms, and her mouth went dry with want.

Miles of tanned skin and hard muscle filled her vision, and the memory of what that flesh felt like entangled with hers instantly brought heat up her chest, neck and face.

"There you are." He padded lightly across the carpeted floor, his steps surprisingly quiet as he did. "I thought I'd misplaced my wife when I couldn't find her in our bedroom."

"Our?" Her brain tried to grasp what he was saying, but she couldn't quite get it to work properly while he was standing in front of her, tempting her to run to him and throw herself at him.

She shook her head, willing her mouth to work. "I didn't think you'd want to sleep in the same bed."

He tilted his head, silently asking her to elaborate.

"We hadn't discussed sleeping arrangements."

He stepped closer to her, cupping her cheek and letting his thumb slide gently across the flesh there.

"Is it not customary for married people to share a bed in America?"

"No, it's just that we aren't the typical couple,

Aléx. I didn't think you'd want me in your bed until we were actively trying to conceive."

He tilted her head back, making sure her eyes were on him and nothing else.

"Were we trying to conceive when I first asked you to join me in my bed?"

She tried to shake her head, but his fingers were buried in her hair, preventing her from moving. As his nails lightly scraped against her scalp, she said, "No, we weren't."

"Then you should know that I expect you to sleep by my side. Are you okay with that?"

It was an impossibility to her how this man managed to be so dominant and controlling and yet still insist on her agency at the same time. It was the only reason she wasn't concerned by Aléx's domineering ways. She knew if she wanted to, she could say no, and Aléx would respect her choice. Did she want to? Hell no.

"Yes." Her voice was husky and nearly unrecognizable to her own ears. How could this man reprimand her and turn her on at the same time? There was something deeply wrong with her that she was this into his BS.

"Are you okay with everything that happened the last time you were in my bed happening again, right now?"

His hand had slid free of her hair, and now his strong fingers were curling around her neck, his thumb sliding against the pulse point at its base. Her heart was beating a loud tattoo in her chest, and she was certain he could feel every beat with his thumb positioned there.

"I'm waiting for an answer, Treasure."

"I'm not ovulating yet. We wouldn't conceive tonight."

He pulled her into him. The hard planes of his broad body fit easily into her soft curves. His length was hard and thick against her belly, and she had to fight herself not to drop to her knees right then and try to swallow him whole.

"My reaction to you wasn't about wanting to conceive then or now, Regina. I simply want you. I've been haunted by our one night together for four unrelenting months. I need to feel you under me again. I need to know it and you weren't a figment of my imagination. Will you let me have you tonight?"

Fire flickered inside her belly from a small spark to the growing inferno she could hardly contain. Did she want him? Did she want him to have her? Hell-to-the-absolute-yes.

"I'm yours anytime, anywhere you want me."

To the novice ear, she was certain she sounded thirsty and pathetic, begging for a man's attention. What they'd need to understand to even remotely comprehend the unfolding scene is that Aléx was no ordinary man.

It wasn't just his body, although Lord knew that was enough. His tanned bare chest, strong and supple with its defined muscles, didn't just represent a hot body to bring her pleasure. It represented a safe place to let go and come undone.

She'd come undone that night in his hotel room; she'd allowed him to erase every care and worry she had and just simply focus on him, to exist in the pleasure he supplied.

"Careful, Treasure." His voice was deep and rich like aged bourbon, intoxicating as it drew her in. "I might just take you up on that."

Regina slid her hands up his arms and down his pecs, loving his warm skin underneath hers. She'd been nearly consumed by that heat all those months ago. There was no way in hell she was missing out on it now. If Aléx was offering to let her bathe in that fire again, to let her forget everything, including the fact that this would be all he could ever give her, she would allow him whatever access to her body he wanted.

"I wholeheartedly expect you to."

There was no warning. Like a lion, he was ferocious and fast, lifting her until her legs were around his hips and his lips were on hers. He drank from her, taking all she had to give and still demanding more.

When she broke away from the kiss to drag air into her burning lungs, she noticed they were no longer in the previous bedroom. They were in his...correction, theirs. She'd stayed in that other bedroom because she hadn't wanted to assume anything between them. Aléx had been clear about love not factoring into their relationship. She'd agreed that it wouldn't be a problem. She was simply here to get the things she wanted: a baby and her hair care line. Couldn't this intimacy be one of those things too?

He answered the question rolling around in her head when he loosened his grip on her and allowed her to slide down his taut body until her feet touched the plush carpeting on the floor. With skilled hands, he slipped one spaghetti strap of her camisole down and then the other.

"The night I came to your apartment, and you walked out of your bathroom wearing a similar set, I had to fight myself not to touch you. You were hurting, and me groping you wasn't what you needed. God, but how I wanted to. That image has been replaying in my head on a constant loop."

He let the silk camisole fall until it puddled around her feet on the floor, stepping behind her before placing searing lips against the base of her neck. It was a simple touch, but instant flames engulfed her as her lust consumed her. He pulled away, forcing a desperate moan from her. She lifted an arm, burying her fingers into his thick, dark strands as she attempted to drag his mouth back to where she wanted it.

"The last time we were together, everything was hot and furious, Regina."

"Are you complaining?"

He was pressed against her back now, and she could feel the soft rumble of a sexy chuckle rolling through his chest.

"Not in the least. Except that I wished I'd had more time to explore every inch of your body. I intend to make up for that now."

He pulled the silk shorts of the set down, slowly setting her skin on fire with each touch. Once she stepped out of them, he stood and cupped her heavy breasts from behind, rolling his thumbs over the sensitive flesh of her nipples. Her body tingled at his touch, need blossoming inside her that every place his fingers grazed, no matter how lightly, made her ache.

He used one hand to pull her face to his, kissing her deeply, his tongue tangling with hers as his free hand slipped between her thighs. She would've gasped if she could, but his kiss was so powerful, so thorough, it seemed to capture her breath, leaving her air-hungry as his fingers found her folds.

Carefully he slid his fingers between them, finding the slick evidence of her arousal, and he moaned so deeply she could feel it reverberate through her body, causing her sex to throb, aching for more.

More of his touch, more of him, more of the need he was stoking in her.

"How could you ever believe I wouldn't want you like this every chance afforded me?"

He slowly stroked her clit, his fingers moving in rhythm with the cadence of his words. Her hips began to swerve to the rhythm he was creating, chasing the pleasure his fingers so expertly gave to her. She was so close, right there on the precipice of release. She just needed…needed…

He slipped a finger inside her. The sensation ratcheted up her desire, causing delicious tension to pull at her muscles, making her sex flex around him. He added another finger, and the stretch was so perfect, adding the last spark she was seeking to ignite the climax that had been just out of reach from the moment he touched her.

His strong arm closed around her waist, keeping her upright as she rode his fingers to completion.

"There's my good girl. You have no idea how much I've missed her, how much I've wanted to see her break apart for me."

Slowly, her cognitive abilities returned through the haze of post-climax bliss.

"Is that all you wanted, to see her come on your fingers?"

He hissed between his teeth as if she'd struck a raw nerve. Point one for her. He might be a king with an obedience kink in the bedroom, but that didn't mean she couldn't drag him to lose his ever-present control.

He turned her in his arms, bringing them face-to-face. His eyes were dark and sinister, like she'd cut the last restraint he had. Good. That let her know she wasn't in this alone. This hunger that burned so bright in her blood, seeping into her flesh and taking control of her mind, wasn't just her affliction to bear alone.

"No," he growled through clenched teeth. "It isn't even the tip of what I've wanted."

He took her hand, leading her up the three steps that led to the platform of the bed. His gaze was fierce and hungry, a predator with his long-desired prey in his sights. "On your knees."

There wasn't a second of hesitation in her response. Her body instantly acquiesced to his command. Her brain didn't have time to think about it. The only thing she could do was give in.

He quickly dispensed with his pajama bottoms, his length springing free. Thick and red with protruding veins that wrapped around it like tangled vines, it slapped against his stomach. He leaned down, taking her chin between his thumb and his forefinger.

"I want that smart mouth of yours wrapped around my cock now."

Again, not the slightest bit of hesitation. As soon as he sat on the edge of the bed, spreading his legs to make room for her as he gave himself one long stroke from his domed cap to his base, she was in position, ready to receive him.

She wrapped her fingers around his base, testing its girth to see if he was as thick as her memory had portrayed or if it was just her imagination. She had not been wrong. He was thick and hard, and so ready for her that her mouth watered.

One lick from his sac to his tip and she was rewarded with a heavy groan. His satisfaction evident, she swirled her tongue around his cap, dragging her tongue through the salty pearl of precum waiting for her.

She took him into her mouth, groaning at their mutual satisfaction. Their bodies were in tune; even four months hadn't been enough to make either of them forget how to please the other.

His hips moved involuntarily, joining the rhythm she'd set every time he slid in and out of her mouth. With each stroke, Aléx spoke through his tight jaw, praising her for the way she pleasured him.

"Don't stop."

"God, your mouth feels incredible."

"I could fuck your mouth all night."

She'd be perfectly fine with that if it kept him impossibly hard with his entire body taut with clenched muscles. She looked up at him, seeing his imminent destruction in the fire in his eyes. It was the only encouragement she needed to keep going, until she winked at him, drawing his fire.

"Shit." He sat up, placing strong hands under her arms and pulling her onto the bed. Before she could get her bearings, she was pinned beneath him with him wedged between her thighs and her hands clasped above her head by his. He slammed his mouth on top of hers, punishing her insolence with the firm press of his lips as he devoured her, licking inside her mouth, sharing their comingled flavors.

He tore his mouth from hers once he'd drunk his fill. His chest heaved as he tried to regulate his breathing enough to speak.

"Do you want me to use a condom?" He must've seen her intended response written in the pinched skin of her brow. "And God help me, if you tell me one more time we can't conceive tonight, I'm going to turn you over and spank your naked ass until you learn to never speak that phrase to me again when we're in bed. I want you, Regina. I want to feel you with no barriers. If you're uncomfortable with that, I will wear a condom."

She could feel her arousal sliding down her leg, and she had to wonder whether it was his threat of a spanking or his stated desire for her that made her so wet. Whichever it was, she was certain of only one thing. She needed him inside her right now.

She tugged her wrist free of his hand, sliding it between them, guiding his cock to her entrance.

"No barriers," she whispered.

The last bit of his control disintegrated into nothingness as he slammed into her. There was no finesse. There were no seductive moves to draw out their pleasure. It was as if her consent drove him beyond reason. The only thing she could do was wrap her legs around his hips and hold on for the ride.

Her muscles clenched around him as each stroke pushed her closer and closer to the incredible gratification only he could give her.

"Aléx, Aléx, Aléx." His name became a litany, a psalm, a sacred hymn that expressed everything she was feeling, everything she couldn't explain, everything she didn't allow herself to think even for a second.

Her climax crashed over her. She buried her

nails in his shoulders, trying to find purchase until it ebbed. But he would have none of it. He kept stroking inside her with such power and intent that another climax dragged her under its powerful waves. She couldn't breathe. She didn't need to. All she needed was Aléx and the incredible way he made her body do his bidding.

"Mine," he growled as he continued to glide in and out of her. "You're mine, Regina. Mine."

His body stiffened as he slammed into her one last time before his orgasm took hold of him. She could feel him pulsing inside her, marking her inside and out.

As they settled and he gathered her into his arms, intertwining her limbs with his, the little piece of herself she'd lost when he'd called her sister's name that first time clicked right back into place. If she was his, then he was hers too.

CHAPTER ELEVEN

REGINA TURNED TOWARD the furnace that seemed to surround her with heat, feeling familiar muscle, skin and sinew. They'd been married for three weeks now. He'd been true to his word, making sure they slept together, as in a euphemism for sex, and slept together, as in actually sleeping together every night.

"Good morning, my queen. Are you going to sleep all day, or should we go out and explore the grounds? I'm afraid I've been a terrible husband by keeping you naked and in bed almost every moment of the day."

"Trust me," she murmured through the haze of sleep and building lust. "A sistah ain't mad at you."

"I guess I should take that as a compliment, then." He pulled her into him, dropping her leg around his and notching himself between her thighs.

"Oh, it definitely was meant as one."

"You tempt me beyond reason, my queen. We

do need to get up, however. I'm afraid we must hold court next week. That means this week, we have to get ourselves and the house in order. The world will not stop just because we've found undeniable pleasure in each other's arms."

She groaned loudly as she buried her face in his chest. "Boo to the world. It sucks."

"It does indeed, Your Majesty."

She peered up at him, finding the easy humor in his eyes. This was the man she'd met that night nearly five months ago. She'd never thought she'd see him again. That was especially true after she'd admitted the truth of her identity to him. But somehow, fate had managed to bring him back into her life, and Regina was enjoying every bit of it and him.

"It feels so weird every time you address me by that title."

With his elbow bent, he held his head up as his penetrating gaze seemed to look through her.

"Weird? Those titles are rightfully yours. You are the queen of Obsidian Island."

That was certainly true. The moment she'd said "I do" and signed the marriage license, all rights hereunto were bestowed upon her. Now if she walked into a room, everyone stopped and bowed or curtsied.

The first time this had happened, she'd stood quietly in awe watching for nearly a full two minutes. Aléx had to whisper in her ear that they would remain in that position until she gave them leave. She'd felt so bad. She couldn't imagine how uncomfortable it was to hold that position for so long simply because she hadn't a clue about her role.

"Aléx, I don't know how to be a queen. And the truth is, I don't want to be one in name only. If I'm going to be here, I'd like to learn your customs and your history, learn about your people and your land. I'll be teaching our children everything I can about Black American history. I want to be able to teach them Obsidian history, and why what their father does matters, too. I want to be the partner you need and the queen that they need. Show me how to be that."

His eyes widened, and his mouth was slightly slack as he stared at her. "I hadn't really thought you'd be interested in any of that."

"My lab won't be ready for another week. Am I supposed to sit around eating bonbons while you do all the decreeing and knighting that I'm sure will take up your whole day?"

The rumble of his laughter sent tremors throughout the bed. Seeing Aléx this way, with his dark hair mussed and his skin flushed from all they'd done in this very bed throughout the night, this unguarded version of him, tugged at her heart.

"You Americans." He shook his head. "Where do you get all these wild notions about what being a monarch actually entails?"

She poked him in the chest with a playful finger. "I told you before, we've got Disney princess movies and *The Crown*. Oh." She snapped her finger and continued. "We've got *Game of Thrones* too. With those poor examples, what do you expect?"

That earned her another laugh, and she took joy in her reward. Aléxandros the king made for a striking picture. Aléx the man, however, was breathtaking in his exuberance.

"All right." He sat up, jumping out of the bed and pulling her by the legs until she was at the edge of the bed. "If my queen wants to be a queen, then I'm going to send you to someone who was trained by the best queen of all."

"Who was the best queen?"

"My mother. And she taught my sister, Eliana, everything she knew."

Regina closed her eyes, trying to remedy the slight fatigue she felt behind them. This always happened whenever she studied something too long. Whether it was looking through microscopes, reading chemical formulas, or—as she was doing now—reading all the materials Eliana had given her to bone up on Obsidian civics, her eyes were the first part of her body to give up the fight when she concentrated too hard.

"You look like you need a break."

Regina looked up to see a smiling Eliana sitting down next to her on the plush chaise in what she'd come to learn was the drawing room. To her, it looked like a big and fancy living room. She figured being royal was so fancy that even her billionaire status meant she was so out of her depth she couldn't tell the difference between the two.

Eliana, princess of Obsidian Island and current heir to the throne should anything happen to Aléx. She was tall, slender, with a full face of flawless makeup and long, dark hair falling in waves down her shoulders. The woman's beauty and poise were indisputable facts. She looked like she'd stepped right out of *Ms. Royalty* magazine to grace the peasants with her presence.

In a smart two-piece double-breasted suit, she more closely resembled someone who was running a Fortune 500 company and less like someone who could quite possibly end up inheriting a country if Regina didn't produce the heir her husband so desperately wanted.

"Do you think you've prepared enough for your introduction to court tonight?"

Regina had tried to forget all about that. It wasn't that she was afraid of being around people. She just couldn't put on airs to save her life. It's why her sister was the face of Gemini Queens, and she worked behind the scenes doing her part to make the company a success in her own way.

"Thanks to you, I think I have all the houses and families down, as well as the different titles for the royals and the aristocrats. Whether I'll end up making myself look like a fool is another matter altogether."

What Reigna offered Jasiri as someone who was well-versed in networking and socializing with the goal of furthering an agenda, Regina would never be able to provide for Aléx. Where Reigna was suave, Regina was blunt. And the first time someone said something that remotely rubbed Regina the wrong way, she was way more likely to curse them out than her cultured twin. Not that Reigna wasn't famous for gathering folks too. She was just a great deal more elegant about it, when she needed to be, than Regina.

"Are you regretting asking to learn what it means to be an Obsidian queen yet?"

Eliana's trimmed brow was lifted into a perfect arch. If it weren't for the teasing smile on her face, Regina would think the woman was taking sadistic joy in her discomfort.

"No," Regina countered. "I'm enjoying learning about your history and its connection to Nyeusi. It's sort of awesome that sister nations now have sister queens."

Eliana's smile broadened. "I hadn't thought about it like that. But you're correct, it is pretty awesome."

"You're sure you aren't bothered by that fact?"

Confusion turned her sea-blue eyes into a darker cobalt as she stared at Regina.

"Why wouldn't I be thrilled about that?"

"Well," Regina began, "if your brother hadn't married me, you'd be the next queen."

Eliana raised a manicured finger, shaking it slightly. "That's only if my brother never married or sired any legitimate heirs. And even if those two things were true, he'd have to precede me in death. Also, you're assuming I want the job."

Regina scanned the woman's face to see if she could discern any artifice. She could find none. The woman was serious. Eliana leaned in, placing a hand on top of Regina's.

"I love my country, but I have never wanted to be its monarch for any reason. I'd sooner give it to Jasiri than take it on myself."

"Jasiri can inherit the throne here?"

"One of the weird things about royal blood is that most royals in the world share some kind of consanguineous connection. In Europe, most royals are related through Queen Victoria. For Obsidian Island and Nyeusi, it's Queen Nairobi."

Regina nodded along as she made the connections in her head. "Jasiri once mentioned the consanguinity part." She opened one of the books she'd been reading and found Queen Nairobi's picture and pointed at it. "Your brother said she was a Nyeusian princess."

"Not just any Nyeusian princess," Eliana clarified. "She was the daughter of a Nyeusian king, which meant her descendants are part of the line of succession in both Obsidian Island and Nyeusi. If the royal line was wiped out on Obsidian Island, Jasiri would have a legitimate claim to the throne. The same is true for my brother and any heirs you and he produce. You could give birth to a future monarch who could claim both thrones."

She took a big, exaggerated breath as if relaying that information had tired her out. "But thanks to you, I will be pushed to the back of the line of succession once you and my brother procreate. On that count alone, you are now my official favorite person in the world. I like fun and chaos too much to want to be the monarch of this country."

Eliana's excitement about Regina's place and purpose concerning the line of succession lightened her heart while simultaneously scaring her to death. What would happen if she couldn't give Aléx, and by extension the nation, an heir?

She could feel panic trying to close its grip around her throat, but she refused to allow it. The best way to combat the unknown was to create a plan using as much viable and pertinent data as one could find. She couldn't science her way into getting her husband to love her. But she could damn sure science her way into giving him the child they both wanted.

"Are you all right, Regina? If I've broken you with all this talk of lines of succession and babies, my brother is sure to punish me by assigning me some dreadfully boring task like listening to a presentation from the minister of agriculture."

That pulled Regina out of battle plan mode and made her laugh until she could feel wetness in her eyes.

"I'm fine. I just need a little help from someone who enjoys fun and chaos and is probably good at getting things in and out of the palace without anyone knowing, especially not the king."

Eliana clapped her hands together, rubbing them in a conspiratorial way that let Regina know her sister-in-law was all in.

"I am your faithful servant, my queen. What does Her Majesty require?"

"I need a bunch of ovulation kits. If your brother and I are gonna make sure you never have to become queen, I need to use science and technology to figure out the optimal time to do that. I just don't want everyone knowing and adding extra pressure on me and, by extension, your brother."

The sharp planes of Eliana's face softened with compassion. Regina figured if anyone understood what living under scrutiny was like, it had to be an actual princess.

"You'll have them in your hands by tomorrow."

Regina had never considered what it might be like to have another sister. She and Reigna were literally two halves of one whole, a built-in second self who would always hold you down no matter what. This woman was showing her that non-twin sisters were valuable too, even if they didn't share any DNA with you.

CHAPTER TWELVE

Regina stared at the negative ovulation test with disbelief. She'd been tracking her ovulation for nearly a week and with no success. Her ovaries had decided to forgo her usual cycle and refused to release an egg.

Since her first period, everything about her cycle had been textbook. A twenty-eight-day cycle starting off with three days of light menstruation. That meant two weeks later, she should've been releasing an egg. It was now three weeks after her cycle and still, every single test she'd taken had said no.

Stress.

This had to be about the stress of becoming queen. Aléx had done all he could to make this transition smooth for her. Her presentation to court had been an informal (for royalty anyway) event in the throne room where only high-ranking members of court were present. He'd also set up an interview with the two of them to introduce her to his people in lieu of an exhausting media tour and in-person events. Still, the added pressure must be getting to her if her cycle was this off.

Disposing of the test in the private bathroom of her new office at her lab, she decided she wouldn't stand there obsessing about this. She'd put in a call to her ob-gyn back in the States. Hell, she'd fly back if the doctor advised an examination. She needed to figure this thing out one way or the other.

It made no sense to involve Aléx until she had facts to help her understand what was going on. Until then, she had this beautiful new lab her husband had built for her from the ground up. She'd lose herself in experiments to calm herself down and keep herself focused.

She worked for hours, formulating, testing, reformulating and retesting relentlessly. She didn't stop until she started to feel hot.

"Damn, working under these lights must be getting to me."

She pulled off her lab coat before grabbing more of the polyethylene glycol to get this next trial underway.

She continued to work until the building ache in the back of her head began pounding, and she had to reach for a nearby stool to sit down.

Just as she sat, her phone rang. The sight

of Aléx's name on the screen made her smile through the throbbing.

"Good evening, Treasure. I was under the impression that my queen would be having dinner with me tonight."

"Of course I am. I still have another hour before I need to leave."

His reprimanding tsk put her on notice.

"You should've left an hour ago if we were going to dine at home."

"That can't—" She looked down at her watch face to see that Aléx was telling the truth. She had missed dinner. That's probably why her damn head was hurting her so bad. "I'm so sorry, Aléx. I got caught up in the lab."

"I guess it's good your sister told me you tend to work so long that you often forget to eat or drink. According to her, it's not uncommon for you to become hypoglycemic when you get caught up in whatever you're working on."

The click of her lab door drew her attention away from the phone. She found Aléx walking through it, holding a large paper bag in his hand.

"You really are amazing. My head is killing me, and I'm feeling a bit dizzy. Whatever you've got in there had better have a decent amount of carbs."

"Will chef's garlic butter pasta, that you love so much, do?"

If her head wasn't pounding, she would have squealed in response. "Absolutely will. Let's just take it in my office. We're breaking all sorts of regulatory statutes by bringing food into the lab."

She stood up, and he held the door for her. When she made to take her first step, her vision began to swim. She glanced up to meet Aléx's eyes and found his face sharp and tight with panic.

"Regina?"

It was the last thing she heard before everything went black.

Aléx was king of all he surveyed. His word was law, and his will was absolute, and yet none of that mattered in this moment. That absolute power he had was rendered useless as his wife lay in the hospital ward of the palace.

Her beautiful rich brown skin looked slightly ashen against the stark white sheets of the hospital bed in the center of the room. She had an IV in her right arm and a blood pressure cuff on her left. There were electrodes underneath the hospital gown she wore with wires protruding out of the collar.

The beeps of the medical equipment joined together like the notes of an orchestra. Only this time, any change or movement in their music could mean a detriment to his wife's health.

He moved from the corner where he was hovering, needing to be closer to her, to touch her, to remind himself that she was still here, still with him.

Nothing in life had terrified him more than seeing her collapse in front of him, her head bouncing slightly off the hard tile of the laboratory floor.

He'd activated the panic alarm on his phone, and within seconds, security was in the room, assessing the situation and calling for help as he'd gotten down on the floor and cradled Regina's limp form into his arms.

Now he slipped her hand into his, startled by how cold it still was. Worry began to assail him again, so he pressed the button for the nursing station in the next room.

The doctor treating her entered. Some, just some, of Aléx's building anger subsided.

"She's been in this bed for hours. What the devil is wrong with her?"

Before the doctor could speak, he heard Regina moan. Her face was scrunched up like she was in pain, and every protective bone in his body wanted to comfort her. They hadn't sent anyone to the block in nearly a century, but if this doctor didn't fix what was ailing Aléx's wife, he was going to lose his head before morning.

"Can you stop barking, your kingship? My head is killing me."

"Treasure?"

She cracked one eye open, and relief bled through him, making his legs feel wobbly. He sat down in the chair next to her bed, never letting her hand go as he used the other to bring the chair closer to her bed.

"Are you okay? You scared the hell out of me when you passed out like that."

She groaned again. "I passed out? I guess that will teach me to let my blood sugar get that low again."

"Your Majesty, I'm afraid it wasn't your blood sugar that caused you to faint."

Regina finally opened her other eye and followed the sound of the doctor's voice until she was staring at him.

"What's wrong with me, then?"

"The ventilation system went out in your lab." The doctor opened the chart in his hand, grabbing his reading glasses from his lab coat. "The emergency technicians found an opened container of polyethylene glycol on your working station. We think the poor ventilation and chemical exposure may have contributed to your fainting."

"No wonder it was starting to get hot in there." Regina rubbed the side of her head, presumably trying to give herself some relief while she spoke. "I was so focused on what I was doing,

I didn't realize. I thought it was the overhead lights at my workstation."

"As I said," the doctor continued, "we think the conditions and the chemical exposure contributed to your fainting, but we don't think it was the cause."

For the first time since she'd woken up, Aléx pulled his eyes from Regina's frail form and looked at the doctor.

"Then what the hell is wrong with her? Go ahead and spit it out, man."

There was a small, cautious smile on the man's lips, and Aléx was two seconds from calling in the palace guards and having the doctor thrown in a dungeon. How dare he find amusement of any kind in his wife's ailing condition?

"Your Majesties, the queen is pregnant."

"The queen is what?" Regina said as she sat up in her bed, grabbing her head the moment she did. "That can't be so. I had my menses as normal. It's been more than three weeks since then, and every time I've used an ovulation kit, it's said I'm not ovulating. How can I be pregnant without ovulating?"

The doctor walked closer to the bed, placing a gentle hand on Regina's shoulder, adding just enough pressure until she took the hint and lay down. He then pressed a button on the side of the bed, raising Regina's head up.

"You probably mistook implantation bleeding for your menses. The reason the ovulation tests were negative—"

"Is that I was already pregnant. Damn, I guess I'm proof that educated fools do exist. How could I be this stupid?"

The doctor chuckled. "Not stupid. Just not looking at the right signs. It happens more times than you'd think. I'll leave the two of you alone so you can talk amongst yourselves. May I be the first to congratulate you both on the coming heir."

Aléx finally found his voice as the shock of the doctor's news wore off, and he finally met his wife's gaze. His heart was pounding with excitement and worry, and if he admitted it to himself, he was all kinds of nauseous too.

"We're going to have a baby."

The words rushed out in an almost disbelieving huff. His chest was tight from the growing ball of joy swelling so quickly that it was pressing against all his vital organs. If dying of happiness was a possibility, Aléx was certain he might be nearing the end. It was a childish game Regina and her sister had played that brought them here. A twin swap gone wrong had brought joy bursting back into his life like he'd never imagined possible. For the first time in five years, Aléx was going to be a father again.

He glanced over at his wife. Her eyes were

filled with tears, and she was looking at him as if he was the strongest, most capable person she'd ever met in her life. When she looked at him like that…goodness, it was more than pride, it was healing, slowly chasing away the darkness that had plagued him for so long.

He wanted to be the man she saw with his whole being. He wanted to be unscared, unafraid, and free to face his past without fear of drowning in it again.

The urge to tell her what she made him feel and what this news truly meant to him clawed at his insides. She was his wife. She should know what he'd been through and why this child was such a gift to him.

He could hear Jasiri encouraging him in his head to tell Regina the truth. Even in Aléx's imagination, his fellow king was just as bold and insistent.

Aléx took a deep breath, preparing to follow Jasiri's advice, trying to convince himself that he was stronger than his past, when the memory of what he'd become when he'd let his grief consume him flooded his mind. Weak, empty, and unfit to take care of himself, let alone an entire nation. Aléx's pain had shredded him into tiny pieces, some of which he'd never recovered.

All Regina saw was the strong man she believed she'd married. He couldn't help wondering what would happen if he shared his truth with his wife. Would she still look at him the same?

Too afraid of losing her favor and too selfish to give up how she made him feel, Aléx decided now wasn't the right time, if there ever was such a thing. Until he could be sure he wouldn't revert to the broken man he was in the midst of his grief, he'd keep his truth locked behind closed doors.

CHAPTER THIRTEEN

ALÉX SAT STRAIGHT up in bed from a deep sleep. His heartbeat thudded in his ears as his lungs gasped for air.

"Mmm, Aléx...what's wrong?"

The sound of Regina's groggy voice coming from the other side of the bed was like a slap across the face. It provided just enough control, just enough clarity for him to pull himself together.

He leaned down to her, placing his hand lightly at the base of her stomach. At sixteen weeks, she wasn't quite showing yet, but he could feel the slight firmness the small swell of their child caused. It was an ever-present reminder that this was real, and he would in fact be a father soon.

He placed a ghost of a kiss on her cheek and whispered, "Nothing, I just need to use the restroom. Go back to sleep."

She covered his hand with hers, its warmth battling with the cold chill his nightmare had left him with. He wanted to stay there, to curl around her and hold on to her and their child until the rays of the morning sun broke through the blinds and started him on his day.

He couldn't, though. Not like this. His heart was still racing, and he was barely keeping his respiration at an even level. Regina would know something was wrong. He refused to burden her with this. Her job was to grow their baby. His was to protect them at all costs. He would not fail that mission.

He slipped out of bed and into the en suite bathroom, closing and locking the door behind him, then turning on the faucet at full stream to drown out the loud pulls of air he was trying to tug into his lungs.

It had happened again. The dream had found him and had nearly strangled him in his sleep. The first time it happened had been after her eight-week doctor's visit where the first sonogram was done. The sound of their baby's heart pounding so strong through the exam room had nearly brought Aléx to his knees with joy.

They'd gone back to the palace and spent the rest of the day in bed. His heart was too full to speak, so he'd shown her his appreciation with every touch, stroke and pleasure he knew how to give to express to her how happy he was to share this with her.

That night, the first dream had come. The crash of water slamming down on a vessel, screams from the crew and passengers. Another punishing wave hitting, tipping the vessel over on its side until it capsized and was dragged beneath the waves into the abyss.

He knew that memory was real. He'd watched those very events happen. But the sound of the small voice saying, "Daddy, save us," was very much a new development. And the worst of it was that the faces of that "us" changed from blond hair, blue eyes and tanned skin to a million nearly invisible dark braids with deep, reddish-brown skin and the deepest brown eyes that had captivated his soul.

It wasn't Regina. It wasn't the child you share with her. They are safe. They are still here.

Paternal anxiety was the name for what he was suffering from. It was when an expectant father had recurring fears about his wife and baby dying in childbirth. It was rather common, especially in expectant fathers who'd experienced a loss.

He washed his face in the sink, hoping the hot water would soothe his nerves. When he caught sight of his reflection, he saw a frightened man with haunted eyes.

He came out of the bathroom, taking a quick glance at Regina in their bed. The rhythmic rise and fall of her chest made a fraction of his fear subside. Satisfied that she and the baby were okay, he grabbed his robe and headed for the only place his scattered mind would let him go.

He walked down the still corridor to the door at the end of the hall. He tried his best not to twist the knob open. He knew there was nothing but pain behind that door. That's why he'd locked it away from him and the rest of the world for the last five years.

Save for the one person tasked with cleaning this room, no one stepped inside it but Aléx. His father had known about it, along with his sister. His house staff knew about it too. There was no way to keep such a thing from spreading among the staff. But they'd all been warned that if they spoke of it in the open, they'd be let go immediately.

While they all knew about the room, with the exception of his father and sister, they'd only known that an old friend with a young child was coming to stay, and Aléx had wanted the visitor and the child to feel at home. Since the existence of the room, Charlie's true connection to him, and what the room held captive behind its doors hadn't shown up in the gossip rags in the last five years, Aléx was inclined to believe the staff didn't know who Charlie was, and they'd taken his threat about losing their jobs for speaking out of turn seriously.

Unable to stop himself, he placed his thumbprint on the scanning panel above the knob, the resulting audible click letting him know the door was unlocked.

Aléx, you are pathologically masochistic.

He stepped inside, the motion light flickering on to show him what he'd known would be there. It was exactly the same as the day he'd closed it.

A platform bed covered in expensive pink frill. A ridiculous number of pink-and-white pillows filling up the top half of the bed.

An antique white rocker settled in one corner of the room. Matching furniture with the same accents and design strategically positioned throughout the room. This included a custom-made vanity whose mirror, surrounded by white painted iron, spelled out "Charlie" in elegant cursive letters.

He'd had this room commissioned the day he'd found out he was a father. He'd taken great joy and care in creating it. Happy fantasies of reading to his little girl in that rocker and tucking her into bed at night had danced through his head with every swatch of fabric he'd selected and every fixture he'd commissioned. When it was finally complete, he'd never been prouder of any other project he'd ever undertaken.

He hadn't known that Charlie wouldn't live to see her perfect princess room. He'd never suspected that one week after its completion, it would go from the surprise he'd hoped to give to his daughter to a mausoleum to house his pain.

His eyes continued to scan the room until he found the picture that had haunted him for years. Sent to him from Farah's phone, Charlie and her mother smiled brightly for the selfie as they boarded the boat he'd sent for them. He'd known from their last conversation that Farah was deeply angered by his commands and threats. But even in her anger, she'd found a way to share in Charlie's excitement at being on a boat for the first time and had thought enough of him to share that moment with him. What none of them had known in that simple moment of joy is that the boat would send his ex-lover and their child to their deaths.

"Save us, Daddy."

"I couldn't, dear one. I couldn't."

His shaky fingers grasped the framed picture, and he pulled it to his chest, hoping its nearness would slow his heart and comfort him in some way. Unsurprisingly, there was no comfort in sight. How could there be when he knew his failure to protect them was the reason they weren't with him today?

He placed the frame back on its perch atop

the dresser and stared at it as if he were talking directly to the people smiling back at him.

"I promise you, I won't let anything happen to them."

Regina stepped outside their bedroom just in time to see Aléx exiting a room at the far end of the hall. His shoulders were drooping as he walked with his head slightly bent, like he was too exhausted to lift it.

Concern drew her in his direction. Aléx was a tall man, well over six feet, and his broad, muscular body made it impossible for him to not take up most of the space when he walked into a room. As he pinched the bridge of his nose, he seemed so small and frail; she worried he might just shrink until he disappeared into the plush carpeted floor.

"What happened?"

His head snapped up at the sound of her voice. For a moment, she could see what looked like sadness floating in his gaze, but by the time she was standing in front of him, his royal mask had dropped into place, and she could see she was no longer standing before her husband. Now, here stood Aléxandros, the king of Obsidian Island.

"Nothing. I needed to check on something for work."

"And it was so urgent that you needed to leave our bed and handle it at two in the morning?"

He walked around her, heading back toward their bedroom as if he expected her to follow without question. That wasn't happening. Something wasn't passing the smell test.

"I'm a king, Regina. I don't work a normal nine-to-five. When duty calls, it doesn't matter how late or early it is."

She stopped walking, crossing her arms as she planted her feet. "And you had to go to an unused bedroom to do kingly work, why?"

"It isn't unused," he snapped at her, the sharpness of his tone sliding across her raw skin like a blade.

Her spine straightened, and the tight set of her jaw must have conveyed he'd crossed a line, because he raised both hands before saying, "It's a secure storage closet for important files. Trust me, it's just dusty remnants from the past. Nothing you need to worry yourself about."

He closed the gap between them, returning to her and taking her hand. He brought it to his lips and kissed it, looking at her through his impossibly long, dark lashes that spread out into an elegant fan above his cheeks.

"Come, Treasure. It wouldn't do for the queen not to get her sleep. You're growing the future ruler of a nation. You need as much rest as you can get."

Something niggling at the back of her mind

insisted she press him. The king, however, was a skilled strategist. When he passed those same lips across hers, she forgot exactly what she was thinking about.

He pulled her against him, deepening the kiss as his tongue pressed until he was licking inside her mouth, stroking her into a frenzy where the only thing she could think was, "More. Please, more."

"Come, Treasure." He laced his fingers through hers and gently guided her toward their room. "Perhaps we both need to burn off this extra energy so we might grasp the few hours of darkness left for sleeping."

She knew she shouldn't. Whatever was happening with Aléx, it had nothing to do with work. Of that she was certain. But letting him stoke her fire until she thought she might explode seemed so much more important in this moment. She'd find out what was going on later in the day. Tonight, she was going to give herself to her husband for as long as he wanted.

CHAPTER FOURTEEN

REGINA BURST INTO Aléx's office. Always in tune with her, he stood up behind his desk.

"What's wrong? Is it the baby?"

"Yes and no," she answered. "At least, it's not our baby."

She held her hand to her abdomen. It had formed into a full baby bump and not the cute little thing at the bottom of her stomach. She had to wear maternity clothes now since their little one had decided to make its presence known.

"Reigna's in labor!" She practically squealed the words. "I need to get to Nyeusi immediately. Can you call for the ferry?"

"You're not getting on a boat, Regina. You're five months pregnant."

She could feel her brows pinch as confusion settled in the deep V between them.

"As far as I know, there's no travel ban on five-months-pregnant women on ferries."

He pressed his hands flat against his desk. "I don't want you on the damn ferry."

The sharpness of his tone cut through her. Aléx didn't make a habit of raising his voice. As a king, he believed wholeheartedly that being ill-tempered could compromise his ability to serve his people. Which was why she couldn't figure out for the life of her just who this man was and just who the hell he thought he was talking to.

"I'm not one of your subjects. Don't talk to me like that. My sister is having her baby, and I'm not missing it. Either you find me a way off this island, or I will. Either way, I'm not missing this."

He blinked, took a breath and allowed some of the tension in his body to bleed out.

"I apologize. I was out of line. I'm just concerned for your safety."

She shook her head.

"Regina, be reasonable."

She folded her arms and tilted her head as she stared at him.

"I know you didn't just fix your lips to insinuate this baby—" she pointed to her bump "—is making me irrational?"

The sharp cut of her eyes must've been enough to convey he was taking his life in his own hands, because he straightened and held his hands up.

"I'm simply saying I just don't feel safe with you on the ferry. I'm an expectant father. Forgive me for being worried about you and our child."

She took in the tight lines around his eyes and mouth. He *was* scared.

What the hell for?

She stepped closer to him, walking around his desk and taking his hand in hers, placing it on the top of her belly.

"We are fine. I understand you're overprotective of us. But I have to get to my sister. It's either the boat or the helicopter. I thought you'd say hell no to the helicopter, so I assumed the ferry would be acceptable. I need to get to my sister now, and I'm going to make that happen however I must."

He nodded, dropping his head in both contrition and agreement.

"The helicopter will be ready to take us in fifteen minutes."

She gave him a cautious smile as she attempted to step away. He pulled her into him, surrounding her in his warmth as he wrapped his big body around hers.

"You and this baby are everything to me, Regina. Everything. Forgive me for crossing the line."

She slipped her arms around his waist, sensing that he needed her strength in this moment. Something was going on with him. Something that had been happening since she'd seen him coming out of that room. There was no proof of a correlation there. But she was determined to find out if there was. First, however, she needed to get to her sister's side. Everything else would have to wait until later.

"Look at Auntie's baby."

Aléx watched his wife holding the new Nyeusian heir. Princess Shadae, daughter of Queen Reigna and King Jasiri of the House of Adebesi, was a beautiful cherub with a head full of dark curls, and she had his wife completely wrapped around her finger.

Regina radiated with joy that shone through the room like a floodlight. The sight of her holding that baby made him ache for the moment she'd do the same with their child in another four months.

Jasiri walked over to Regina, holding his hands out as Regina leaned down to get one last snuggle from the princess.

Jasiri was well over six feet, like Aléx, and just as broad as him too. The sight of this hulking man cradling his daughter like a fragile piece of glass soothed something in Aléx. The ache that had dogged him for five years was still there. But in this moment, its tentacles didn't squeeze him with the same strength they regularly did.

"Cousin, would you like to hold her?"

His head told him to say no. He shouldn't intrude on this wonderful moment with the new princess.

"It is customary for the monarch of Obsidian Island to bless the Nyeusian heir apparent on the day of their birth and vice versa. Your mother did it for me, and my father did it for you. You wouldn't rob my daughter of experiencing that honor, would you?"

Aléx looked into Jasiri's eyes and saw hope and the cunning of a king. It was true, this was a custom shared between their people since the birth of King Nikos and Queen Nairobi's firstborn. King Amir traveled from Nyeusi to bless the new heir. When the next Nyeusian king had a child, the Obsidian king paid the same honor in return.

Jasiri was doing this on purpose, to pull Aléx out of the hell he'd lived in for five years. The arrogant bastard knew Aléx would never be able to refuse him this request.

Jasiri placed the tiny bundle in Aléx's arms and stepped back once he was sure his daughter was secure in Aléx's grasp.

"Did you forget your standard?"

Aléx couldn't take his eyes off the tiny human he was holding, not even to answer her father.

"No," he said, as the baby made reflexive sounds. "It's in my satchel. It occurred to me you might not want me to do the ceremony considering we haven't been close for a while. However, I brought it anyway figuring it was safer to have it and not need it than to need it and not have it."

Baby Shadae squiggled like a bowl of gelatin until Aléx repositioned her, placing her head in the crook of his arm and hugging her to his body.

When he looked up, Jasiri had removed the large flag with the Obsidian royal crest on it. He handed it to him, waiting in earnest for Aléx to begin.

Aléx glanced back down at the baby as she burrowed like a cat until she found her sweet spot in his arms. Without even realizing it, Aléx was smiling as his insides softened.

Is this what children did? Did they sand down your rough edges until they were smooth to the touch and were no longer a danger to you or anyone else? He hadn't been around enough children to know if that were true. Not even the child he'd fathered.

Before he could allow his painful past to encroach on this moment with this sweet child Jasiri had entrusted him with, he wrapped the standard haphazardly around the babe before he took a deep breath.

He glanced up at his wife, her eyes glazed over in reverence as if she were imagining him holding their baby in the future. His throat felt tight with emotion, because he couldn't help but imagine that himself.

"Princess Shadae, daughter of Queen Reigna, issue of the great King Jasiri, standard bearer of the House of Adebesi, heir apparent, and crown princess of the Nyeusian throne."

He slowly swiped a reverent thumb across the child's head before he spoke again.

"May you possess the wisdom of all your ancestors so that you will rule with forethought and foresight."

He flattened his hand on the babe's chest, the rapid tattoo cinching his heart with an imaginary thread that seemed to be connecting them.

"May your heart be filled with compassion and kindness, so that you will rule with grace and benevolence."

He plucked a tightened fist from beneath the standard and gently opened Shadae's hand with his thumb.

"May your hands be as open and strong as your heart so that you may carry and comfort your people and your nation through the sorrows life will inevitably bring."

Shadae chose that moment to kick her leg free of her blanket as if she'd come into this world knowing what her role was. He took the tiny foot into his large hand, marveling at how delicate it was.

"May your feet be strong and sturdy, so that you may stand as a beacon to your people in times of light and darkness."

He readjusted her blanket so that her foot was covered and she wouldn't get cold. He looked up at Jasiri, his cousin nodding as he watched Aléx honor his daughter. There was pride in his eyes, and abounding love. Maybe it was wishful thinking, but Aléx dared to think just a little of that love Jasiri was exuding was for Aléx himself.

Aléx knew he didn't deserve it. He didn't deserve the loyalty Jasiri showed in keeping his secret from Reigna, and therefore Regina, either. That didn't stop him from wanting to be part of Jasiri's inner circle. Perhaps the birth of this little one was a means to let Aléx's walls down so he could embrace this man again.

His heart full, he lifted the baby to him. Leaning down, he placed a feathery kiss on her forehead.

"To Princess Shadae of the House of Adebesi, may your reign be long and may your legacy live on forever."

Jasiri motioned to the sisters, and they each joined him in repeating after Aléx in unison.

"May your reign be long, and may your legacy live on forever."

The new princess opened her eyes for the first

time and looked up into Aléx's face, giving him a reflexive smile. From all the books he'd read, Aléx knew logically that she wasn't intentionally smiling at him. And yet it still made his heart soar.

He walked over to Reigna's bedside and handed her the baby. Before he could step away, she squeezed his hand to garner his attention.

"Thank you for honoring my daughter."

"It was my pleasure, dear queen."

He stepped back to where his wife sat with the wet remnants of her tears on her cheeks. She motioned for him to lean down for a kiss. Their lips lightly pressed together before he tried to stand up, but her firm hand on his shoulder kept him in place.

"Aléx," she whispered. "You're going to be a great father."

From his wife's mouth to God's ear. After holding that precious babe in his arms, every fiber of his being wanted her words to be exceedingly true.

CHAPTER FIFTEEN

"Your Majesty?"

Aléx turned his head toward his secretary, who was sitting before him, attempting to review his schedule for the day. This was something that happened every day he sat in his office, and yet he couldn't seem to focus on anything the secretary said.

"I'm sorry, Michael. Could you repeat that, please?"

His focus had been shot to hell since he'd held Princess Shadae in his arms a week ago. He and Regina had spent two days on Nyeusi, celebrating the newborn with her parents and grandparents. It was two days of bliss, where Aléx hadn't been dogged by the constant ache in his soul that seemed to be a permanent reality of his life.

"The Queen's Ball is quickly approaching, and I haven't yet received any notice from the queen or the princess regarding themes and guest lists. The invitations must go out in the next ten days if we expect donors to attend."

Confusion settled over him. How could this be? The annual charity ball, given in his mother's honor to supplement the education ministry's ability to keep postsecondary school free on Obsidian Island, was one of the royal family's most important events of the year. Without it, so many scholars who didn't have the benefit of wealthy parents would be left behind. His mother believed that the best minds, regardless of who they were and what tax bracket they were in, should have access to quality education. Obsidian Island would only thrive if its thinkers were diverse and brought different ideas and experiences to help address their nation's problems.

How had he let this happen?

He knew the answer to that. He'd been so preoccupied with thoughts of the new baby, her smell, the warmth growing inside him when he held her, and how happy it made him seeing Jasiri in his new role.

That last part was what surprised him most. Aléx had never questioned the distance between him and Jasiri, only accepted that it was there and moved on with his life. But now, Jasiri seemed to be trying to breach the chasm that had existed between them for nearly two decades.

"Michael, in light of the queen's condition and her still learning about all things Obsidian, please contact the princess. I wish for her to partner with my wife to make this year a phenomenal one in both attendance and donations."

Michael nodded quickly before standing, bowing again before he took his leave.

As soon as his office door closed, Aléx's mind fell back to his distant cousin and the new heir. Before he could stop himself, he dialed Jasiri's number, hoping he'd answer and not send his call to voicemail like Aléx had done to his over the years.

"Good morning, Cousin. How fares the king of Obsidian Island on this beautiful day?"

Jasiri's jubilant tone drew a genuine smile from Aléx, one he was certain Jasiri would be surprised by if he had witnessed such a thing.

"Spoken like a man who is deliriously happy with his new daughter."

Jasiri chuckled. His deep, rich voice sounded lighter than Aléx had ever heard it.

"You are right on both accounts. I am deliriously happy with my new daughter. I'm also just plain delirious because the princess has mixed up her days and nights, and Reigna and I aren't thrilled at the idea of bringing in a nanny."

"You're forgoing a nanny?" That wasn't something he'd ever heard of in royal circles. His parents had certainly raised him, but there was no way they'd been able to keep him and his sister underfoot while his mom was queen of a nation.

"Not exclusively, no. We just want to have these first six weeks or so with Shadae until we feel we've all bonded more completely."

Jasiri's words resounded in his heart and head. It sounded absolutely terrifying doing all the preliminary work of taking care of a newborn yourself. As much as fear seemed a reasonable response, the thought of hoarding that initial time with his wife and their child sounded like heaven. Could they do it? Would Regina want it? Would their child be the better for it?

"Jasiri, aside from the new-father euphoria, you're all doing well, aren't you?"

There was a pause, and Aléx wondered if he'd gone out of bounds by asking something so personal. They weren't close. Perhaps he didn't have the right to an answer.

"We're doing well. It is difficult, especially with so little sleep, but I wouldn't trade it for anything. My daughter is everything that is good in the world. You'll see what I mean when your child is born shortly. Everything seems irrelevant but the well-being of that precious life you've been charged with caring for. If you're half the man you believe yourself to be, you'll do everything within your power to ensure your baby has the best you can offer. I do it for my little one, and I have no doubt you'll do it for yours when they arrive."

There it was again, that same tension of hope and fear mixed together that had him wondering if he wanted to cry or laugh or both.

With his throat tight, he managed to say, "Thank you, Jasiri," leaving the silent *I don't deserve your generosity* off the end.

"Now that I'm king…" Jasiri seemed to change the subject without any transition to what this new train of thought might be. "I can see just how important it is for the sovereign to rule from a place of joy and reverence. I think you know what I'm talking about."

Aléx knew exactly what Jasiri was referring to. He'd started out his reign that way. Even though his ascension had meant the loss of his beloved mother, he'd found a peace and appreciation that he could do as his mother had trained him and take care of their people in the wake of the loss of their queen.

But a handful of years later, that peace, that joy, had changed into something darker and more elusive. It was only his sense of loyalty to his mother, that understanding that he could not fail her, that made him climb out of his abyss and be a king to the people his mother loved.

"Aléx, just know I'm here." The weight of Jasiri's words sat on his chest like an immovable boulder, making him work for each scrap of air he managed to suck into his lungs. "When you're ready to tear down this damned wall between us, when you're ready to let me be there, I'll be bulldozing it from the other side."

"Jasiri, I—"

"No excuses or explanations. We are blood. In Nyeusi, that means something. I know it means something on Obsidian Island too."

His tongue was heavy, and Aléx's awkward ineptitude when it came to letting people get close to him made him retreat into his usual snark.

"Our bloodlines aren't as intricately tied as you'd make it seem. We both know if we hadn't married identical twins, any children we had could've been the next Obsidian/Nyeusian pairing in our combined royal lineages."

Instead of cursing Aléx as he no doubt deserved, Jasiri laughed loud and full.

"Aw, you can try to be mean to me, but it won't work. I've missed you all these years. I could definitely use the wisdom of a man whose governance over the last eight years has been aspirational. But more than that, I want my friend back."

"You sure about that?" Aléx's question might have been delivered with the hint of sarcasm he always seemed to exude when he was talking to Jasiri. "I was the one who distanced myself, first out of sheer jealousy, and later out of shame."

"Jealousy," Jasiri repeated, as if Aléx's statement was an impossibility. "What could you have possibly envied me? We grew up the exact same. Two boys groomed from birth to lead their nations."

"Except your father let you be a boy and then a man. You were raised to believe being king was only part of who you are. I was raised to understand it was an identity that I couldn't escape. That's what I envied, your ability to be you. Outside of being king, I'm not really certain who I am."

Aléx stopped a minute, trying to consider if he should share his vulnerability with anyone. It was always a risk for a king to let down his guard in front of anyone. Doing so could be weaponized against him if he chose the wrong confidant.

"I thought I was beginning to figure that out when I learned about Charlie. But just like that, she, and any inkling of who I thought I could be, vanished."

Aléx closed his fist around the edge of his strong oak desk, waiting for his insides to shatter the way they did the last time he'd tried to vocalize what that loss had felt like. After more than a beat, it didn't come. Instead, there was a sliver of relief that seemed to break through the concrete slab that barricaded his feelings.

"You're not just a king, Aléx." Jasiri's words eased into his consciousness as if the man were dealing with a scared animal. "You are a good man, even if you're a bit obstinate at times. If you weren't a good man, there's no way Regina would've chosen you as her husband and the father of her future children. Your wife is, quite frankly, scary smart. There's no way she didn't calculate a million and one different outcomes before she agreed to marry you. In all her calculations, she concluded you were the one she wanted. The question is, when are you going to start believing that she made a good choice?"

He had certainly made a good choice. His wife was so patient with him, even when he was acting like a right bastard. Regina was turning out to be the source of peace and joy in his life. Maybe he could start to be the same for her.

"You said the first reason you'd distanced yourself from me was jealousy, and the second shame. How does shame factor into all of this?"

If admitting he was jealous of Jasiri's allowed freedom was difficult, admitting his deep shame felt nearly impossible to Aléx. His habit of hiding himself from the world was still there, but somehow it didn't seem to have as strong of a grip on him as it usually did.

"The night they died," Aléx began slowly, "you saw me at my worst. I was broken and destroyed. My pride probably would've recovered if I'd been able to deal with their deaths in a healthy way. But the fact that I had a mental breakdown that had to be covered up by my father and sister made me feel less than. I was the king who had been strictly trained to put the crown first and never let my feelings impact my ability to rule. I thought poorly of you for the freedoms you indulged in. I thought you were the lesser king. But then my mind collapsed in on itself, and I could hardly breathe on my own, let alone rule. How could I face you knowing you saw me like that?"

Jasiri was so quiet, Aléx had to look at the screen of his phone to make sure the call wasn't disconnected. He heard the loud sound of Jasiri taking in a breath before the man spoke again.

"You were my friend. No matter the fact that we hadn't spoken in years at that point, it was my greatest honor that you chose to let yourself go in my presence. You did that because you knew I would understand and that I would protect you no matter what. There was no reason then or now for you to fear being vulnerable in front of me. Just as back then, all I want is to be there for you, Aléx. I didn't want you to suffer alone. You chose that for yourself."

The truth of Jasiri's words smacked Aléx in the middle of the chest like a wrecking ball.

They hollowed him out, making him look down for the pieces of his soul the force had fractured. Aléx was the reason for his own isolation. How could he have missed that all these years?

"Aléx, you decided to be alone. You don't have to make that same choice now. You don't have to do this work by yourself. Let your wife be your soft place to land as you put the past behind you. Tell her, Aléx, before it's too late. Don't let her find out from anyone else why you're so lost and afraid and why you especially need her in this moment. She's having your child. She deserves to know the truth."

There was no disputing what Jasiri was saying. He did need to tell her. He just didn't know if he could. Would there be anything left of him if he bared his soul to her? Could he relive that nightmare again? The truth was, he just didn't know. The even greater truth was, he was afraid to find out.

CHAPTER SIXTEEN

REGINA LOOKED AT the door at the end of the corridor, wondering if today was the day. Aléx had left the island for business, and she knew there was no time like the present to do what she'd been aching to do.

She stepped into the corridor, looking back over her shoulder before she headed in the direction of that locked room her husband absconded to when he thought she was sleeping.

She moved quickly, getting to the door and looking for cameras, although Aléx had assured her there were no cameras in the living spaces; they were instead only trained on the entrances so their privacy would never be intruded upon.

Boy, did she hope that was true. If it wasn't, she anticipated having a lot of explaining to do later.

There was some sort of unholy control this room had over Aléx, and Regina intended to find out exactly what it was. When Aléx was with her he was attentive and kind. But every time he came back to their bed after visiting the room, she could feel the tension bubbling off him. He was scaring her. But also, he was messing with her precious sleep that was already compromised by the kicking inhabitant in her womb.

She placed her hand on the knob and tried to turn it. When it didn't so much as shift, she blew out a frustrated breath.

You had to know it wasn't going to be that easy, didn't you?

She was about to try again, leaning down to get a look at the locking mechanism to find out whether the lock could be picked. Not that she herself knew anything about picking locks. She was, however, from Brooklyn, a place where necessity became the generator of resourcefulness to thrive in an environment that wasn't always conducive to doing so.

She was about to try again when she heard, "Regina, what are you doing?"

The sound of Eliana's voice made her jump back, nearly losing the tenuous grip she had on her balance at almost six months pregnant.

"I was… I was…"

She saw Eliana's waiting expression, the one that said, *I know exactly what you were doing*. Instead of cowering because she'd been busted, she leaned into her conviction that she needed to know what was behind that door if she was to protect her husband and their union.

"I was trying to get inside this room. I've caught your brother sneaking out of bed at night when he thinks I'm sleeping. Whatever is in there is taking him through it, and I want to know what this invisible enemy is."

Eliana's face softened, her bright blue eyes fading to a muted gray-blue as the happiness seemed to be leaking out of her.

"If you want to know what's in there, you're going to have to ask my brother."

Frustration, dark and ugly, began to grow inside her chest. Now more than ever, Regina understood she needed to know what was behind that locked door.

"Is this some royal version of snitches get stitches? If it is, it was juvenile back when I was a kid in Brooklyn, and it sure as hell is problematic now when I'm trying to help my husband."

"I know you are." Eliana moved closer to Regina, placing a compassionate hand on her shoulder. "You will never know how grateful I am to you for recognizing there is a problem and trying to figure out how to help. But this is something that belongs entirely to my brother. I will not violate his trust even if I think I'd be helping him by doing it. You must understand that, being a twin?"

God, did she. More times than not, she protected Reigna's trust with her complete loyalty at every turn. Knowing that in her head, however, didn't make her heart ache any less.

Accepting she wasn't going to get anything out of her sister-in-law, she resigned herself to the fact that she'd just have to address the matter with Aléx.

Aléx rushed into the palace, heading for his quarters. He'd left early this morning on what was supposed to be a two-day business trip. The separation anxiety and the need to be with his wife had set a fire under him, and he'd made sure to complete all his work so he could return home by nightfall.

As soon as he opened the door, he found her sitting in the family room on the comfy couch that had become her favorite spot to perch on as of late.

The flicker of light across her face told him she was watching television. If he knew his wife as well as he believed he was coming to, she was probably watching some kind of true crime or murder mystery.

He'd never know why she found those horrid things so addictive, and he didn't want to think about the implications of her ravenous appetite when it came to such shows. Instead, the only thing he could do was stand there and smile at the vision she made.

He walked into the room, making loud thumping steps so she was aware of him entering.

"Goodness, I've missed you, Treasure."

He sat down beside her and stole the kiss he'd been dreaming about all day. Her kiss was sweet and salty, probably remnants of the chocolate-drizzled popcorn she couldn't seem to get enough of. He wasn't sure if it was the taste of the treat or the taste of the treat on her that had him captivated. Whichever was true, Aléx would buy a lifetime supply of it if it meant he was privileged enough to experience it like this whenever he wanted.

She pulled away from him, her full cheeks and her slitted eyes nearly touching because of the satisfied smile on her face.

"It appears you did. Although I'm not sure why. It can't be the nightly trek I make you take to the freezer to get me butter pecan ice cream."

He stole another kiss. This time it was a quick peck, but it was still just as delicious.

"I'll have you know that I live to serve my queen in whatever capacity she deems fit. Those nightly treks, as you call them, bring me immense happiness."

His heart was alight with amusement and joy. Rich and bold, his ability to live in the moment became more and more corporeal as he connected to his wife.

He couldn't quite answer why that was. The truth was, he hadn't even attempted to consider it. He just knew that he liked himself when he was with her, and more and more, he was grateful she'd accepted his proposal. He shuddered to think what he might have become if she'd stuck to her original no.

"Just how, pray tell, do you plan on servicing your wife tonight, oh wise king?"

"Every possible way my depraved mind can think of."

He undressed her quickly, too hungry to take his time. He burrowed his face in the crook of her thigh, loving the heady scent of her there. He needed inside her in the worst way. Before he allowed himself to take her, he would first make certain she was satisfied.

His lips kissed around her folds, waiting for her to spread her legs and make space for him. It didn't take long. He licked her seam, thrilled to find her arousal coating her skin and now his tongue. Too eager to please her, he continued to lap at her clit as he slipped one and then two fingers inside her. The way her muscles were rippling around his digits, he could tell she was right where he wanted her, so close to the edge that a soft wind would push her over the cliff.

"Come now, Treasure. Don't keep me waiting. Give me what I want."

She mewled so prettily it was almost his undoing. Later, he'd have to decipher why her acquiescence made his dick so hard. Presently, however, the only thing that mattered was watching her splinter at his command.

Regina would be beautiful in a burlap sack. But lying on the sofa with her legs spread and her glorious braids fanned out on the arm of the chair, she was the epitome of wanton need that had him ready to come in his pants like a schoolboy.

He gently lapped her sex, allowing her pleasure to ebb. He unzipped his pants, pulling them down just far enough that he could take his wife without causing damage to himself.

He coaxed her onto her knees and positioned himself behind her. Her bump was just large enough that him rutting against her in the missionary position wasn't comfortable for her any longer. Since then, he'd made sure to have her in every position that she could tolerate. This, with her head down and her ass in the air, had become their favorite.

"Brace yourself, Treasure."

She held on to the arm of the chair as he entered her from behind. It was as if her body were made for him. Her sex molded to the exact shape of his length to give him the perfect amount of friction against his sensitive skin. As a reward, he angled his hips to hit that spot she adored, and together they surrendered to this unrelenting need they couldn't seem to quench.

"Treasure," he huffed. "You feel like silk wrapped around me."

That garnered a needy moan from her, signaling that she was close to another climax. He sped up his pace. Having her come while he was buried inside her was only ever outmatched by when they came together. As if on cue, her body began to tighten as he stroked her hard and fast, racing to meet her at the finish line. When she clamped down on him as the first wave of her climax came, it was as if she were drawing his release out of him.

That first jet inside her was sheer bliss, pulling him into nirvana right here on earth. He stroked them both through their mutual orgasms, holding on to her as a lifeline in this sensual storm they'd created.

She was his and he was hers. He knew that as well as he knew his own name. What he didn't know was where this invisible thread that made him want to be with her every moment of every day had come from. He didn't understand what it was. There was only one thing he knew with absolute clarity concerning this matter.

He liked it.

* * *

He held her next to him, breathing in the calm that seemed to rise from her skin. Just being next to her settled every demon inside him. It especially settled those demons he wasn't completely free of.

He knew he should tell her what those demons were. He was ninety percent sure he would feel better if he did. Living like he was torn between two worlds, those of the living and the dead, made it impossible for him to settle completely in either space. Five years ago, he'd thought he'd deserved to be one of the walking dead, still alive but numb to anything that made life worth living.

Now that he had this woman in his arms, and she was growing their baby inside her, for the first time in five years, he felt his heart beating again. So what was holding him back? What was keeping him from opening up to her?

Fear. It was the only truthful answer.

What if she blames you the way you've been blaming yourself for years? What if she takes away the new warmth flowing through you whenever you see her or think about her? What if your confession sends you right back to the abyss you were trying so hard to climb out of? Or worse, would she think his inability to move beyond his past was connected to whatever feelings he possessed for Farah? Would telling her the truth make her feel like she was living in someone else's shadow yet again?

The mere thought of that last question made him wince. He could never knowingly put that kind of doubt in her head, not when he'd seen firsthand how such thoughts impacted her.

The questions ran through his mind on loop every time he thought about speaking his truth. As selfish as it was to keep things from her, the alternative, the risk, it was unthinkable.

Jasiri's warning about someone else telling her echoed through his head, and Aléx had to bite his lip to keep from saying, *impossible*. His sister and Jasiri were the only two people on his side who knew who Charlie was to him. His former head of security was the one who'd dug up the information and made Aléx aware that he was a father. Trusting the man with his secrets and his life, Aléx had sent him to collect Farah and Charlie and bring them home. He'd carried Aléx's secrets to his watery grave.

The only other people who knew were Farah's immediate family. They'd assisted her in keeping Charlie a secret from him. They'd gone as far as secreting her out of the country before Farah's pregnancy could be known or documented on Obsidian Island. They would never betray her by telling the world she'd given birth to the king's illegitimate child. Well, most of them wouldn't. There was one among them who was mercenary enough to completely disregard Farah's desires. But even this individual had to know Aléx would use his considerable power to make them regret that miscalculation for the rest of their life.

Comforted by his assessment of the chance of Regina finding out from someone other than him, he pulled her tighter into his embrace and welcomed the familiar sensation of her body snuggling into his. This woman was his lifeline, and he couldn't gamble with that, not for anyone or anything. Not even for her.

CHAPTER SEVENTEEN

REGINA STOOD BEFORE the mirror in awe. She'd had glam teams work their magic on her before, but this was next-level. She was seven months pregnant, and all her natural curves were deeper and more profound. From her pregnancy boobs, to the swell of her belly, to the deep curve of her hips, everything was on display.

She wasn't at all distressed by the changes in her body. Her pregnancy boobs were a thing of beauty, and Aléx hadn't been able to keep his hands off them. She'd gloried in his attention and her body's ability to both build a human and keep her husband's tongue wagging. Her voluptuousness notwithstanding, the idea of shoving all these goodies into a formal evening gown gave her pause.

She'd called her cousin Amara, who was one of LaQuan Smith's favorite clients. The famed designer from Brooklyn had talked to her for a few minutes and within a week had sent her sketches of dress ideas. She'd picked a bodice from one, a silhouette from another, and before she knew it, she'd had the final product hand-delivered by the designer himself.

As she stared at herself in the large antique mirror in her walk-in closet, she was amazed by that man's talents. He had managed to create an off-the-shoulder, sweetheart-bodice, short-sleeved gown that hugged her curves and made her look like one of the Greek muses, with a chiffon cape to boot. He'd also managed to make it out of some sort of magical material that was stretchy, but elegant, so it would still fit in the event her growing baby decided to add more inches to her already protruding waist.

The design was magnificent, but the bloodred color was very much giving sexy goddess. And she knew from experience that as soon as Aléx got her alone, he'd peel it off her like a second skin.

That thought warmed her until she thought about what was likely to happen the moment she'd undoubtedly fall into postcoital sleep. He'd sneak out of bed and walk down the hall and spend hours in that room.

Before, those visits were infrequent. They occurred enough that she was still concerned after she'd tried to sneak into the room herself without success. Now, it seemed the closer she got to delivery, the more his visits had increased. At this rate, with four weeks to go before her anticipated delivery, he'd probably move into that room instead of sleeping with her.

It was all so confusing. Aléx was the most attentive person she'd ever had in her life. He anticipated her needs before she even realized she wanted something.

Like the time he noticed her rubbing her back when she woke up in the morning. She'd hardly had time to realize the weight of the baby was starting to pull the muscles in her back. The next thing she knew, he was bringing her a C pillow and a belly brace.

Though she hadn't worked in her lab since they'd discovered she was pregnant, she did still go to her office to further develop her formulas and meet up with her marketing team. When she returned to the palace tired with aching feet, he'd be waiting on the sofa with a pillow at one end, patting his leg until she placed her feet in his lap.

For a man who hadn't done much manual labor in his life, he sure as hell knew how to rub a foot. Within minutes, the aching in her soles melted away, and she was relaxed enough to fall into a dead sleep.

Then there was the time her sister told him he had to fulfill her food cravings or it would mark the baby. In response, he'd had a minifridge and freezer moved into their bedroom so he could satisfy her butter pecan cravings more readily. She'd tried to tell him that was a Black wives' tale, all superstition and no fact. It hadn't mattered. He'd done it anyway, because she was giving him the greatest gift. The least he could do is make sure she had the ice cream the baby seemed to have an addiction to.

Goodness, he was so damn caring, and yet he still kept her at arm's length when it came to whatever was going on in his head. One moment, she'd think they were crossing that imaginary line he'd drawn between companionship, care and love. The next, he'd firmly shut the door on her, letting her know she would never truly be part of his inner circle.

Talk about emotional whiplash. Add to that her pregnancy hormones, and she was on an emotional roller coaster the likes of which even Vivian Green couldn't fathom.

"Your Majesty, it is time to don your crown."

Regina turned around to find Janice, a tall young woman with auburn hair that she kept pulled into a tight bun. She was one of the personal staff members Aléx had assigned her. She found Janice to be pleasant, courteous, and above all, punctual. So if she said it was time for her to get the diamond-encrusted headband secured to her head, Regina needed to sit at her vanity and have it placed now.

Aléx chose that moment to enter their bedchamber. He was dressed in what she'd come to know as his king's uniform: a black tuxedo with a cape attached at his shoulders. The breast pocket of his jacket was adorned with military and royal insignias, and his red sash tied his regal look all together, making one breathtaking picture.

He carried a velvet pillow in his hands that held a full diamond crown with what looked like the largest, clearest rubies she'd ever seen in her life. When he stood beside her, she had to fight the instinct to run her fingers across it. Yes, she wanted to touch it, but it was so beautiful she couldn't bring herself to dull its brilliance with even a partial fingerprint.

She looked up at Aléx, trying to recognize the look on his face. His features were straight, but beneath the polished look, she could see his jaw ripple and his eyes brighten with hope.

Hope for what? She couldn't discern.

"This isn't the same crown you presented to me when you introduced me to your court."

"No." His voice was thick as if he were trying to fight the emotions simmering just beneath the surface from breaking through. "This is the crown made specifically for my mother's coronation. It would thrill me to no end if you'd agree to wear it tonight."

She was about to speak when she saw Janice's

reflection in her mirror. What Regina had to say was for his ears only.

"Janice, would you please excuse the king and me?"

Janice gave a quick bow of her head before she disappeared, leaving no trace that her presence was ever in the room.

When Regina looked at the crown again, a lump formed in her throat. Forgotten was its physical beauty; she was too overwhelmed by its sentimental value to be concerned with that.

"You want me to wear this?"

"I do." He gifted her with his million-dollar kingly smile, and she wanted so desperately to get lost in it.

It would be so easy if she could just accept that Aléx couldn't love her. He'd told her that from the very beginning. But every time he did something thoughtful and caring for her, her stupid heart just wanted to dive headfirst in love with him.

"Shouldn't your sister wear it? She's Queen Carisse's daughter."

He placed the crown down on top of her vanity, then stood behind her, placing his hand firmly on her shoulders as he looked at her through the mirror.

"Do you not want to wear it?"

She closed her eyes, wishing it were that simple.

How do you tell the kind man who treats you

like you are in fact a treasure that it hurts every time you let your guard down, when he moves closer to you, only for him to pull away each time?

Bluntly, like you do everything else.

Why her conscience was such an asshole she didn't know, but she was throwing it major internal side-eye right now. That didn't change the fact that it was right, however. She needed to be clear with Aléx. She needed to draw some boundaries.

"It's a beautiful crown, Aléx, and I'd be honored to wear it. It's just, I find it hard to believe you would share something so personal and sentimental with me when you won't even share with me what's going on with you."

His eyes widened, and she realized she'd sideswiped him with her question.

See? her conscience rang out in her head. *I told you blunt was the way to go.*

Ignoring it, she stood, forcing his hands to drop from her shoulders, and turned to face him.

"Regina—"

She held up her hand to stop him. If he started talking, she'd go stupid listening to that smooth-as-silk voice of his. Then he'd kiss her, and she'd lose full control of her faculties. It wasn't happening today.

"I'm worried about you, Aléx. You're barely

sleeping, and you're sneaking out of our bed more frequently."

He raised a brow, confusion pulling his smooth skin into taut lines on his face.

"You noticed that?"

She swallowed, refusing to back down now, even if it made her sound pathetic.

"I always notice when you're gone. Don't you know that by now?" His mouth hung open, so she continued. "I feel safe and protected when I'm with you. Since that first night you held me in my bed after my fight with my sister, I never sleep as well as when I'm in your arms."

"Regina, I'm—"

"If you say 'I'm sorry,' I swear I will find your scepter and bop you on the head with it. I don't want your apologies. I want to help you through whatever the hell is going on with you."

She could see his constitution breaking, falling chip by chip. But just as quickly as he let the wall drop a little, he slapped spackle on it and started layering one emotional brick at a time right before her eyes.

"I ca-an't, Regina. I want to. I just can't."

She closed her eyes, trying to strengthen her legs to keep her upright in this moment. Refusing to let him ruin all the hard work her glam team had done on her makeup, she took a deep breath and sat back down in front of her mirror.

"You can. You just won't. It's your way of showing me you care about me, just not enough to share all of yourself with me. I guess I should've taken you at your word when you told me you'd never love me. Because if you did, you'd know how much watching you suffer would kill me, and you'd do anything to stop that pain for me."

He placed a hand on her shoulder, and she shook it off. She was honestly too tired to deal with this anymore.

"If you'll excuse me, I need to finish getting ready for the ball. I'll wear your mother's crown. So, you can go now."

Aléx snapped his head back as if she'd slapped him. As a king, he probably wasn't used to being dismissed. Well, he'd have to get used to it, because she was tired of him trampling over her heart. From now on, she'd stay in the place he'd given her. Companion and coparent and nothing more.

She watched him out of the side of her eye with his shoulders slightly bent like he had lost just a bit of his strength and a whole lot of his kingly luster.

There her stupid heart went again, wanting to call him back and hold him until her Aléx was back. That, however, was the problem. He wasn't ever *her* Aléx, and he never would be.

CHAPTER EIGHTEEN

Aléx followed Regina's form throughout the room. For someone who said she hated people, she certainly did have the ability to command an audience. She was stunning in her gown. With his mother's crown upon her head, she looked the part of a queen who knew her power.

It was just an act, however. That's all it could be if she didn't know how much he cared for her, how much he craved being in her presence.

His confession was on the tip of his tongue. He'd wanted so desperately to just let the truth slip into the air.

Then what stopped you?

He'd asked himself that every time he replayed the hurt in her eyes when she asked him to leave her alone. Every time, he came to the same conclusion. There were only two reactions he could imagine her having. The first was pity, the second, disgust. Either way, he couldn't stand the thought of her associating either of those emotions with him.

The alternative wasn't that much better. Watching her hurt and close herself off from him was cutting him into tiny pieces, and he didn't know if he'd be able to tape himself back together again.

"Things are not well between you and your queen, are they?"

He closed his eyes at the sound of Jasiri's voice. Of course he and his ever-observant mind would call the situation for what it was the moment he saw it.

"What did you do, Cousin?" Jasiri prompted.

Aléx turned narrowed eyes on Jasiri and found the man waiting for him expectantly.

"How do you know it's my fault?"

Jasiri didn't even try to hold the knowing chuckle in. "I know you too well, Cousin. Of course this is the result of something you did." Jasiri took a long gaze at him before he said, "Or more accurately, something you didn't do. You haven't told her, have you?"

Aléx used that moment as an opportunity to snatch a champagne flute from a passing tray and downed it in one swallow.

"You see that look in your eyes," Aléx countered. "The look that says, 'The poor little king. He's so pathetic with grief and loss that he can hardly function.' I refuse to be viewed by my wife in the same way."

He saw understanding cast a shadow on Jasiri's deep brown skin. He of all people should understand exactly what Aléx meant. When Aléx had received news that the ship had gone down on the border of Obsidian and Nyeusian waters, he'd called Jasiri when he couldn't reach his father and begged him to allow Obsidian naval ships to search inside Nyeusian waters.

He recalled how panic had pulled through him like a taut rope. He was wound so tightly in it, he could hardly think, and he'd lost all eloquence and poise.

Jasiri had heard the panic in Aléx's voice, and even though they hadn't spoken in years, he not only granted Aléx's request, he met Aléx on the water with Nyeusian ships and divers in tow to help with the search. He'd stood on Aléx's ship with him and had held him when he'd collapsed to his knees when his captain announced they'd discovered the bodies of Charlie and her mother.

"I don't want to be that man again. I don't want Regina to know how broken I am. I don't want her to know it was..."

He couldn't say the words. He couldn't make himself say them. Jasiri placed a strong hand on his shoulder, squeezing tightly enough to make him wince, intentionally dragging him out of the fog of grief that was trying to cloud his mind again.

"It wasn't your fault, Aléx. You told her not to travel because of the storm, and she insisted."

Aléx shook his head. "It doesn't matter that I told her not to travel that night. They were only on that ship because I'd demanded to see Charlie immediately or I would use all my power to make Farah's life a living hell. She knew I wasn't lying, so she risked the trip for fear of what I'd do if she didn't make it at the assigned time. No matter how you try to clean it up, I'm the reason they're dead."

Jasiri squeezed his shoulder again before he moved to Aléx's side. He looked out over the balcony they were standing on, watching the people milling about beneath them in the ballroom.

"Aléx, I tried to carry the fear and utter panic I had when my uncle was targeting Reigna's life. I wouldn't let her in, and I tried to make her a prisoner within the walls of the palace. The only thing trying to handle all that pain and fear by myself did was push my wife away until she chose to leave me over watching me devolve into rage and insanity."

Aléx snapped his head toward Jasiri, searching the man's face for any hint of an untruth. His sullen face and his ticking jaw were better than any lie detector in creation: Jasiri was telling the unvarnished truth.

"I didn't know she'd left you. I know she

played a hand in trapping Pili in America. I just never realized she was there because she'd left you."

Jasiri pursed his lips. "No one does. Not even my parents. It's not exactly something I wanted in a royal press release, if you know what I mean. I nearly lost everything that I loved. We didn't know it yet, but Reigna was pregnant at the time. If I hadn't gotten myself together, I could've missed out on watching her grow with our daughter. I could've missed how our love deepened once I had her in my arms again. If I hadn't found a way to be honest with myself and my wife, if I hadn't found the sense to listen to her instead of acting as if I had everything under control, I would've lost it all."

At that moment, Reigna looked up from the ballroom as if she'd felt her husband calling to her. She raised her eyes and gave him a warm, broad smile that seemed to make Jasiri stand taller.

"Open up to her, Aléx. Let her love heal you."

"Regina doesn't love me. We both agreed that bringing love into the equation was a bad idea."

Jasiri fell into a big belly laugh, no doubt at Aléx's expense. Frankly, it was beginning to get on his nerves.

"I'm sure that's some nonsense you came up with and Regina went along with."

Aléx shook his head like a recalcitrant child. "She doesn't love me, and I don't—"

Jasiri interrupted Aléx. "Don't even speak that lie into the ether. That woman loves you. She'd shower you with it if you let her believe she had a chance of you accepting it."

Jasiri pointed to where Regina was standing, talking to one of Aléx's ministers.

"You haven't taken your eyes off her for a single moment of the conversation we're having. That is not the behavior of a man who isn't obsessed with his wife."

"She's pregnant with my child, Jasiri. Of course I'm always concerned with her well-being."

Jasiri shook his head silently.

"Strange, then, that you were looking at her just as intently on your wedding day too. She wasn't pregnant then, was she?"

Jasiri knew she wasn't. Regina had more than likely shared with her sister that they'd unknowingly conceived on their wedding night.

Could the words his irritating cousin was speaking be true? Love? Is that what this impossible feeling was in his chest that made it hard for him to breathe every time he had to leave her? Is that why his body went up in flames any time he touched her, or she touched him? Is that why the thought of losing her and their child the way he had Charlie and her mother nearly paralyzed him with fear?

He took measured breaths, trying hard not to have a panic attack right there on the balcony. For one, it would be all over the news before the last guest left. Second, he wouldn't give Jasiri the satisfaction of gloating.

"Tell her, Aléx. She loves you. She'll understand. Telling her will make dealing with your loss better and will stop you drowning in your pain. Let her be your life raft and your anchor."

Jasiri slapped a hand on Aléx's back as Aléx watched his wife. He wanted to, he needed to, be with her. He'd just decided that he would tell her when he saw Katia whisper in Regina's ear. The two women disappeared through the south doors on the other side of the room from where Aléx and Jasiri were standing.

He didn't know what that was about, but he knew trouble when he saw it.

"I've got to get to her now."

"Katia, whatever this is about, I'm tired and really not in the mood."

The woman held her hands up in surrender as she stepped toward Regina, leaning down closer to her ear to speak. "One of the aides just asked after you. She was called away by another staffer as she was about to enter the ballroom."

Regina eyed her carefully, and Katia gave what appeared to be a genuine smile. "Listen, I know when I'm beat. I can't say I'm happy about it. But I'm also not stupid enough to do something to the queen that could land me in prison for the rest of my life."

That made Regina chuckle. Of all the things Katia had said, Regina believed self-preservation was the woman's first priority.

"Did you see which way they went?"

Katia led her to the foyer and pointed her in the direction of the kitchen. Regina turned around to get another glance at Katia. They'd probably never be friends. But she could respect a woman who could acknowledge her losses as well as her wins.

She nodded and walked toward the kitchen, finding it abuzz with activity. There were people zipping around everywhere until they noticed Regina's presence. At that moment, everyone stopped and bowed their heads.

"Please, don't let me stop you from your work. I was told one of the staffers was looking for me."

A young woman in her mid-twenties stepped out of the frenzied bustle in the kitchen and into the corridor. She dug in the pristine white apron that rested against her black uniform dress and pulled out an envelope that she then handed to Regina.

The envelope's heft and texture spoke of its quality. Her name was scribbled on its front in what looked like perfect calligraphy.

Regina lifted her head to the aide with a pinched brow before she met slightly nervous eyes.

"Who left this for me?"

CHAPTER NINETEEN

ALÉX FINALLY MADE his way through the throng of people that had delayed him from getting to his wife. By the time he made it through the south doors, he saw Katia walking back toward the ballroom.

He stopped abruptly in front of her.

"What the hell have you done? Where is my wife?"

Katia's face twisted into confusion.

"She went to the kitchen to find a staffer who was looking for her. After that, I have no earthly idea."

"Katia." He ground out her name through his clenched jaw. "So help me God, if you've done anything to hurt her."

Katia's neck snapped back in shock as she glared at Aléx. "I'm pushy and I might go too far sometimes, but I'm not violent, Aléx. I wouldn't try to physically harm a pregnant woman."

Her eyes misted over as they moved from side

to side in an anxious fashion. As if she were trying to tell him he should know better.

He put space between them, letting some of the tension bleed out of him. "I'm sorry, Katia. Please, go and enjoy the rest of the party."

When Katia was gone, he traced Regina's steps to the kitchen and back upstairs to their living quarters. He took the steps two at a time to get there. Considering the last thing they'd said to each other, her being out of his sight made him uneasy. He needed to fix things.

He called out for Regina once he made it inside their quarters. The rooms were silent, too silent. Fear ricocheted through him as all sorts of imagined scenarios ran through his head. He shook his head, trying to free himself from the dark thoughts that would paralyze him if he allowed them to.

And that's when he saw it: the soft light coming from that room at the end of the hall. To his horror, Charlie's room door was open. A shift in the air behind him made him aware he wasn't alone. He turned to find his sister standing there with worry written into the lines of her face.

"I swear I didn't think she would react this way, Aléx."

"React what way?"

"I didn't think she would leave when I…"

His mind filled in the blanks, coming to the only conclusion he could. "Eliana, you gave her the key?"

"She was hurting, and you refused to tell her the truth and stop her pain."

His sister had always pushed the boundaries of respectability, but never anything like this.

"It wasn't your place. It wasn't your truth to reveal."

"I'm sorry, Aléx. I was trying to help the both of you. I can't watch you hurt anymore, and I won't watch you hurt Regina in the process. Hate me, banish me if you must. I just couldn't stand by and watch you destroy the best thing that's ever happened to you. I was there when you lost it all before. I can never watch you go through that again."

He could see the hurt in his sister's watery gaze and her trembling lips. His pain had impacted so many people, and he'd selfishly only concerned himself with his own. He grabbed his sister in a hug. He'd deal with his anger later. Right now, he just needed her to feel the love he had for her. After sacrificing so much for him, that's the least she deserved.

"Go find her and bring her back where she belongs, Aléx."

He locked gazes with his sister and nodded.

"I promise I will."

* * *

"Your Majesty, this is the head of security. The queen is at the docks. She's on the ferry to Nyeusi. We're holding clearance until you get there."

"Is my helicopter ready?"

The docks were a thirty-minute drive from the palace. The helicopter would cut that down to ten minutes.

"The pilot has been notified and is making his way to the helipad. However, King Jasiri's helicopter is ready to take flight immediately. He says he's waiting for you."

Aléx ended the call and headed toward the car in the courtyard. Jasiri didn't say a word to him once he'd boarded. Instead, he instructed his pilot to take off. Before Aléx knew it, they were landing atop the roof of the ferry depot directly across from the docks.

He went to step off the helicopter, but he stopped. He grabbed Jasiri into a tight hug and yelled, "Thank you, Cousin," hoping he could hear Aléx among the whirring of the helicopter blades.

He jumped out of the helicopter and quickly made it to the docks. Just as Regina was about to walk inside to the seating area, he grabbed her arm and said, "Not like this. Please, don't go like this."

***

His grip on her arm was tight. She was about to pull away from him until she looked into his stricken face and saw his pale skin and his pinpoint pupils that were locked on to her.

He's scared. No, he's terrified.

She didn't understand this. She had expected concern, possibly anger that she'd dared to leave him, but not fear.

And then he spoke words that doused any anger she'd harbored.

"Not like this. Please, don't go like this."

He looked so unlike himself. He wore the same tailored clothes, but they appeared crumpled and disheveled, as if they were a signifier of the panic she saw covering him.

"Regina, I promise you, if you want to leave, I will have my pilot take you to Nyeusi first thing in the morning. But please, please don't leave me like this. I couldn't survive it if something…"

He let the rest of his words die off in the silence. Nonetheless, she was certain he'd intended to finish that sentence with the words, *happened to you*.

Puzzle pieces clicked into place as she read between the lines.

"They died on a boat, didn't they?"

He couldn't seem to speak. Instead, he gave a single nod as an answer. His breathing started coming fast.

"Please," he stammered. "Just don't—" Again he couldn't finish his sentence. He was almost frantic with fear and nervous energy. This man was truly afraid. Seeing him like this, it broke something in her. Suddenly she forgot how hurt and angry she was, and she found herself pulling him into her arms, holding him and rubbing his back in an attempt to get him to calm down before he started hyperventilating.

"I'm fine. The baby's fine. You don't need to be afraid. I'll get off the ferry."

He held her tighter. His body was literally shaking in her arms. This was so out of character for Aléx. He was always calm to the point he was almost stoic. Yes, he'd come out of his shell more as they'd spent more time together. Never, not one single time in the eight months of their marriage, had he ever come this undone in her presence.

He stood there holding her for a long time until he could get himself together, and then he took her hand and helped her onto the dock.

"I promise, I won't stop you if you truly want to leave. I just need you to give me a chance to explain before you make up your mind. I know I don't deserve it. But I'm not above begging for that grace."

There was a car waiting for them, and he helped her inside before he walked around to the driver's side and got in. The drive was silent, both too afraid to break the fragile truce that had her agreeing to return to the palace with him.

Truly, there was no other choice. He had looked as if he were going to explode with fright if she'd refused to get off the ferry. With how anxious he was, she truly believed he wouldn't have survived if she left on that boat before he'd had the chance to stop her.

He drove with one hand, keeping the other clasped around hers as though he were afraid she would float away if he weren't acting as her anchor.

From the time they exited the car, he took her hand again. He directed her down a path that would keep them away from the guests they'd left in the ballroom. It led directly to their private quarters.

She'd expected him to stop in the drawing room, but he didn't. He kept walking down the corridor until they were standing in front of that door that had changed everything in the blink of an eye.

He placed his thumb on the keypad, and the lock clicked loudly. He gave her hand a squeeze, as if to tell her to prepare herself, before he held the door open and let her walk in, following quickly behind her.

He grabbed the picture frame before he walked

over to the rocker in the corner, motioning for her to sit.

Refusing to let her hand go, he used his foot to position the ottoman right in front of her so he could keep hold of her. It was as if he needed this connection, partly to remind himself she was still here, and partly because he was afraid of her slipping away.

"As the heir to the throne, there are so few choices you have about your life. Who I'd become, where I'd go to school, how my coronation would be planned, even my funeral. All these things were known to me from the moment I can remember being conscious about who my mother was and, by extension, who I would be."

She wanted to reach out to him, soothe the sadness in his voice. Yet she somehow knew if she interrupted him, he might not ever be able to tell her this story to its completion.

"The only thing my mother wouldn't allow to be chosen for me was my bride. Jasiri's father had won his fight against arranged marriages when he married Jasiri's mother. She thought that her son should have the same choice."

He looked up at her, giving her a weary smile before he continued.

"I met Farah and her sister my last year of my graduate program at university. The three of us were great friends and we became comfortable around each other. They were part of the aristocracy, so like me, they knew they had to be wary of what kinds of friends and connections they made, because there was always someone waiting in the shadows to take advantage.

"Of the two sisters, it was Farah who hated everything that had to do with life at court. Her sister, on the other hand, didn't share the same reticence. As time went on, I began to distance myself from her sister because it became clear that she didn't just have an affinity for court. She was angling for something greater, to be the next queen. As a result, my friendship with her sister faded. I thought that would mean losing Farah too, but our friendship deepened. We sort of just fell into this comfortable pattern that led to us dating seriously."

"I bet her sister didn't like that."

The slight curve of his lip confirmed her suspicions. Apparently, Regina and Reigna weren't the first set of sisters to upend this man's life.

"Two years into our romantic relationship, I proposed. It just made sense that we would marry. We grew up in the same world. We both preferred to be out of the limelight. We got on fabulously. But when I asked for her hand, she said no. Two days later, I went to find her to try to convince her to change her mind. Her sister told me she'd left the day before, and the family had no idea where she'd gone."

"Don't tell me her sister decided then was her chance to shoot her shot?"

He did that thing again where he silently mouthed her words to make sense of them. She loved that he did the work of applying basic context clues to understand her Brooklyn and her AAVE. It was often hilarious, but she loved it all the same.

"She did in fact 'shoot her shot,' as you say. She hasn't stopped shooting it since then, no matter how many times I tell her it will never happen."

It was time for her to puzzle the pieces together until his words solidified their meaning in her head.

"Katia is Farah's sister?"

He closed his eyes and let his head sink in emotional exhaustion.

"Tell me the rest."

He laced their fingers together, rubbing his thumb against her skin, causing electricity to flow through her. It tethered her to him, connecting them on more than a physical level. He was drawing strength from her.

"Less than a year later, my mother died, and I became king. Two years after that, my head of security walks into my office and tells me he has news. Apparently, when you become king, at least in the first few years of your reign, royal investigators search for threats to the monarchy, including but not limited to illegitimate children. Evidently, right around the time my mother died, Farah had a baby. My baby."

She could see the weight of those words bearing down on him, cutting through to his core. It made her squeeze his hand in return, a silent reminder she was here.

"I confronted Farah. Came down on her with the full weight of the crown. I demanded she bring my daughter to me, or I would take the child from her because she'd stolen the girl from me. She tried to explain that she'd kept Charlie a secret because she didn't want her to have to live as my bastard child at court. I reminded her that Charlie wouldn't have been illegitimate if Farah had married me like I'd proposed. She said she couldn't. A gilded cage was still a cage, and she didn't want to feel imprisoned for the rest of her life."

His eyes began to redden as he continued.

"I was so pissed with her. She'd stolen my daughter from me. Charlie was born three weeks before my mother died. She robbed my mother of knowing her grandchild. I gave her a week to return to Obsidian Island. If she missed the deadline, I would have an arrest warrant issued for her. She was on Nyeusi, with whom we have an extradition agreement. She knew I had the power to realize those threats, so she agreed."

The anger slid away, and sorrow crept in. She could see the ache of loss begin to eat at him, and she wanted so badly to comfort him, to tell him it was all right. But she couldn't. She couldn't ignore this thing that had been cutting him to the bone and taking more and more of him away from her and their baby.

"The day she was to leave, weather reports warned of a coming storm. As soon as I learned of it, I told her not to leave, that she could come after the storm without penalty. But she was so angry with me for forcing her hand that she wouldn't listen. She told me she'd already packed up her place, and she was leaving early enough that the storm shouldn't be an issue. They'd be here in an hour."

A single tear slid down his cheek as he looked at her, reaching for a lifeline to help him get through this last part. The worst part.

"The storm came early."

The impact of those words hit her square in the chest.

"They lost control of the vessel."

Again, another thump in the middle of her chest as the staccato of his cadence beat against her like a drum.

"The boat capsized, and they were lost at sea. Search teams from both Nyeusi and Obsidian Island implemented every rescue plan available.

Soon, however, rescue turned into recovery. They were gone."

She reached out for him, pulling both his hands into hers and pressing her lips against them.

"Dear God, Aléx, I'm so sorry for your loss."

His head snapped up as his gaze landed on hers.

"My loss? You don't blame me?"

Regina was a very smart woman, there were few things in the world that she didn't understand or couldn't figure out easily if she dedicated her attention to them. This, however, had her stumped.

"Why on earth would I blame you? It was an accident."

He shook his head and stood up, pacing back and forth in front of her.

"Because of my selfishness, my need to reclaim what was mine, I led the three-year-old daughter I'd never met and her mother on a path that ultimately led to their deaths. This is my fault."

She sat back, trying to take him in, seriously trying to follow his logic, and she couldn't. She just couldn't. Too raw from all the emotions of the night, she just didn't have the stomach for any of what was happening. There was only one way she could handle this situation and him. She would shoot straight from the hip.

"That is bullshit, Aléx, and you know it. Are

all kings this arrogant, or is there some sort of stupidity gene that runs in royal bloodlines? I swear, between you and Jasiri, I don't know who has it worse, me or my sister."

"I beg your finest pardon." He stopped dead in his tracks and looked directly at her.

"Listen, you and Jasiri spend a whole lot of time taking on the weight of the world and thinking that the women in your lives can't handle it. Everything is on you. News flash. You are a king, not a god. You have no more control over the weather than I do my bladder at night when your kid is tap-dancing on that organ like it's Savion Glover, Gregory Hines and Sammy Davis Jr. all wrapped into one."

He stood with his mouth hung open, and she figured he was either too shocked to speak or having some sort of brain aneurysm. Either way, she figured since she'd already pressed her luck this far, she might as well keep going.

"It was a tragedy, Aléx. There was nothing you could've done to save them."

She walked over to him, poking her finger in his chest in hopes the discomfort might bring him out of his apparent stupor, because he still hadn't responded to her.

"You had every right to demand Farah bring your daughter home. I don't care what her issues were with being at court. That did not give her the right to rob you of being a father. Her dying doesn't absolve her of that."

She put one hand on her hip and jabbed the air with her finger as she spoke. She was so damn pissed. This man, this kind and caring man had wallowed in pain for five years because of someone else's action.

"There is no one to blame for their deaths, Aléx. It was a terrible, terrible accident. But that's not what all this guilt is really about, because you know there is nothing you or anyone else, including Farah, could've done to stop this."

His shoulders stiffened as he asked, "What are you saying?"

"I'm saying you don't blame yourself for their deaths. You blame yourself because you can't find it in your heart to be angry with a dead woman, so you'd sacrifice your own soul to avoid the truth. You're mad as hell at Farah for keeping your daughter from you. Had she not died, I have no doubt you would've made her very aware of that fact."

She threw up her hands, hoping the gesture would help her message break through to him.

"Here's another news flash, Aléx. You have every right to lay that particular blame at Farah's feet for lying to you all those years."

He stood there just watching her, taking in her heaving chest as if he couldn't recognize her in this moment. That's because he hadn't had the opportunity to meet protective Regina. This was who'd threatened Jasiri, warning him not to hurt her sister or his ass was hers. And she didn't care that Farah was dead. She wasn't letting her slide after watching her husband suffer so much guilt that he couldn't sleep at night.

"You're out of line, Regina. What the hell do you expect me to do? Just forget them and move on with my life as if they never existed, never mattered? I'm grieving, Regina."

His pain reddened his tanned skin, making him look like he was burning from the inside out. He was in a hell of his own creation, one he had no clue how to leave.

"You're no longer grieving, Aléx. You're punishing yourself because you lived. You are allowing your past guilt to rob you of joy in the present. I would never ask you to forget them. They are part of you. The problem is, you're making them all of you, leaving no room for yourself, me, or this baby."

She grabbed his hand and laid it on her stomach, holding it there, hoping it would be enough to bring him in from the cold.

"I need you, and this baby needs you, and I'll be damned if we lose you because of your misplaced guilt. I love you too damn much for that. So, here's how this is going to go down."

She stepped around him, walking toward the door before she looked over her shoulder at him.

"I'm tired. I'm tired of holding back, and I'm tired of pretending that I don't love you. I have more than enough love to keep the three of us afloat while you dig your way out of this abyss. But I've got to know you are trying to free yourself of this. Now that I've said my piece, I'm going to put on some comfy fuzzy pajamas, eat some butter pecan ice cream, send off some emails to my team to firm up the launch of my hair care line, and take myself to that ridiculously big bed of ours and go to sleep. Do whatever you need to grab hold of the truth, and if I find you in bed with me tomorrow morning when I wake up, I'll know that you've chosen to live in joy with me rather than suffocate in guilt."

She turned, her shoulders drawn back as she waddled down the hall. The ball was in his court now. She'd laid everything on the line. He knew where she stood, and she knew she couldn't allow herself to watch Aléx be consumed by his guilt any longer. It would kill her. For her sake and their baby's sake, she had to force his hand. He had to make a choice. Settled in her conviction, she refused to acknowledge the twinge of worry that asked, *What if he doesn't choose you?*

She knew the answer. She'd hurt like hell. It was as simple as that.

CHAPTER TWENTY

Aléx stood in the graveyard as his eyes scanned the cold double headstone that read, "Farah & Charlie, Together in Eternity."

By rights, Charlie should have been laid to rest in the royal mausoleum. Though she would never have been able to rule because of legitimacy laws, her parentage meant she should have rested beneath the palace where all the monarchs and their children were interred.

When Farah's family requested they be buried together, Aléx had not been able to deny them. The thought of his daughter alone, without the one person she depended on her entire life, seemed unnecessarily cruel.

Since their burial five years ago, he'd not been able to visit this space. It was too strong a reminder of what he'd lost. It augmented his self-recrimination and made it impossible for him to function on the most basic levels. But today, he had to be here. For once in his life, the cost of his guilt was too high a price to pay.

"Farah and Charlie, I must apologize to you. I have allowed my remorse to twist your lives and your deaths into something ugly that neither of you deserved. You deserved to rest in peace and not have my pain poison your memories. You deserved loving and happy thoughts that would've tied your legacies to love instead of pain. I wronged you so terribly, and I hope that you can find some way to forgive me."

The wind whistled lightly through the air, and Aléx had to wonder if it was just nature, or the two souls he was talking to letting him know they could hear him.

"I too must find my way to forgiveness. I need to forgive myself for taking on the blame of your deaths." He turned his head to the left, looking specifically at Farah's name chiseled into the ornate concrete slab. "And Farah, I need to forgive you too. All these years, I blamed myself for your deaths so I wouldn't let my anger toward you rise. You stole the most precious thing in the world from me. You made a selfish decision without consulting me, and as a result, I never had the chance to meet my child. I couldn't admit that until a very blunt woman made me face that fact last night."

He could look back on Regina's words with muted amusement now. Last night, however, he hadn't found them the least bit funny. He was still too mangled by his guilt to see reality.

"I love her, Farah. In a way I never thought I'd be able to love a woman. She pulls out these gnarled old parts of me and buffs them to perfection until they are shiny and new. I've been so afraid to love her for fear of losing her and for fear of disrespecting your and Charlie's memories.

"It's been hard for me to see this, but she made me realize love doesn't have to be an either-or situation. It can be a both-and. I can mourn your loss and still be angry with you for what you did to me. I can hold the love I had for you and Charlie in my heart and still love Regina and the child we've created completely."

He kneeled, swiping his hand across the cold stone and smiling reverently at it.

"So I've decided that's exactly what I'm going to do."

Tears filled his eyes, painting the headstone in a shimmering cascade. He cried for the loss of their lives. He cried for the loss of his opportunity to know and love his daughter. And then he cried for the hurt he'd caused himself, but most of all, Regina. He cried until he was empty, and the only thing left inside him was hope. Hope for a tomorrow he'd never dreamed he could see.

He pulled his handkerchief from his inner jacket pocket and nodded to them, but more so, to himself.

"I'm going to honor the two of you by loving her boldly and honestly, and by being the best father I can to our baby. I'm finally going to let the two of you rest in peace."

A gentle breeze connected with his cheek as if a hand were cupping his face, acknowledging what he'd said and encouraging him to follow through.

Suddenly light with hope, he stood, bent into a bow to show his reverence, and then he turned toward the car. His wife and child were expecting him, and he'd be damned if he'd keep them waiting any longer.

She fought hard not to wake up. The moment she rose, she would have to face whether her husband chose his guilt or her and their baby and the life they were supposed to be building together.

Even with the blackout curtains drawn, she could tell the new day was upon her. She could also tell something else.

Her husband was not in the bed with her.

Refusing to hide, she pulled herself up and leaned her back against the massive headboard. Her eyes were still closed as she made a running list of the things she would have to do now.

Contact a divorce attorney.

She was married to a king. Could she even get a divorce? Charles and Di and Andrew and Fergie divorced. There had to be a way she could rectify this mistake. It was one thing for her to marry a man knowing he would never love her. It was something altogether different to know he couldn't or wouldn't love her because he'd rather hold on to crippling guilt than accept the love she wanted to give him.

Look for a place to live on Obsidian Island.

They might be splitting up, but she wasn't leaving. No matter how her heart hurt, she would never take their child from him. She wanted Aléx to be an active, present parent.

Staying on Obsidian Island would be hard. She knew that. She would miss every second she wasn't with that man. Aléx had somehow embedded himself into her bones, and freeing herself from his hold was not going to be easy. She'd have their baby. She'd also have her work and her lab. She'd stayed up much later than she intended trying to numb her mind with work. Her line, Obsidian Queen, was set to launch six months from her due date. Now she was transferring leadership to her assistant in preparation for her maternity leave. Aside from distracting her from her hurt and worry, hopefully the work she was putting in now would keep the launch on schedule. Apart from their child, her hair care line might be the only thing she had left to keep her going if things didn't work out.

Relief bled through her as she thought of her work. She'd made certain the entire deal she'd made with Aléx gave complete, irrevocable ownership to her. She'd spent most of her working life in a lab. The wheeling and dealing part of business just wasn't for her. But she'd picked up enough from watching her sister and their Devereaux cousins to know how to protect her assets and interests when it came to signing contracts.

Her forethought meant she could be independent here, something she'd come to treasure. She'd never regret working with her sister all these years. Having something of her own...it meant she was finally learning who she was. And deep down, Regina was strong. It would hurt, leaving this man she loved so desperately. Yet she had no regrets. She'd done all she could do. He'd made his choice, and now they would all have to live with it.

"Are you done making your list in your head? If you are, I've got your morning cup of orange tea and this godawful apricot jam you insist on putting on your toast."

She kept her eyes closed but couldn't stop the happy tugging at her mouth that demanded she let the biggest smile she'd ever shone cut loose.

"Don't knock it 'till you've tried it. Your kid is on this fruit kick that's got me in a chokehold."

She heard him settle the tray on the nearby nightstand before he crawled into bed beside her, pulling her into his arms until she became the little spoon to his big spoon.

"It was my intention to be here when you awoke."

He held her tighter, as if he were afraid she would slip through his fingers at the first opportunity.

"Then why weren't you?"

"Because I had to take some time alone to say goodbye. I went to their graves and paid my respects."

Her hands clasped around his, making her strength available to him if he needed it. She'd seen him at his most vulnerable last night, and her protective instincts, where he was concerned, made her want to fight the world on his behalf, even if that included him.

She held her breath as she waited for him to continue, knowing whatever words he spoke next would be the most consequential of her life.

"I told them that I loved them, that I would never forget them. I told them I had to live, that I wanted to live, so that I could love you and our child completely."

She let the breath she was holding escape through pursed lips, her lungs deflating like overextended balloons.

"I thought I could do this without loving you, Regina, and I was wrong."

He lay there with her, letting his words hang in the air, letting her soak them all up. Like a menthol balm to achy muscles, those words melted in her flesh, seeping deep into her soul.

"I should've known I was wrong when I woke up in my hotel room alone and I had to fight myself not to follow you back to America and drag you back home with me."

If he'd thought waking up without her had been difficult, he should've tried leaving. She'd had to force herself out of his hotel room because she'd known if she stayed, she'd never be able to walk away. Knowing he was suffering just as much gave her a perverse kind of joy. It was petty as hell. But at least she wasn't alone in her misery.

"I should've known it when I wanted to murder someone because I thought the woman who'd thoroughly ruined me was marrying Jasiri."

What she and her sister had seen as a harmless lie had such a serious impact. Aléx's confession was proof of that. She would forever regret the anguish he'd suffered as a result.

"If I could ignore all those things, I should've known how deeply I'd fallen for you when you collapsed in your lab." His arms tightened around her even more as his body tensed against hers. Even talking about this still affected him.

"The thought that you could be seriously hurt, that you might leave me..." He couldn't finish the sentence, but the hard and fast tempo of his heart against her back made her understand how that incident had terrified him. "And once we learned you were pregnant, it triggered all my fears about Charlie and her mother."

That surprised her. She turned in his arms to face him, a feat that wasn't exactly easy at eight months pregnant.

"What are you saying, Aléx?"

He cupped the side of her face, and she burrowed into it, loving his warmth, needing it to get her through whatever he was about to say.

"The reason I couldn't sleep at night wasn't because I was mourning them, Regina. I couldn't sleep because I kept having dreams that I would lose you and our child just like I had them."

"Aléx."

Her heart pained her, thinking of the agony he'd been fighting through alone.

"You couldn't have known, Treasure. I wouldn't have let you know. I was so determined to be the suffering hero of my own story. Talking to you felt like letting you down. I was afraid you'd either pity me or hate me. Either way, I couldn't tolerate you thinking of me in either sense. Not when I knew what it was like to be held in your esteem."

Her eyes watered, and her tears spilled onto her face. He immediately wiped them with his thumb, smiling down at her.

"Treasure, I will never hurt either of us like that again. Seeing you on that boat put things into perspective for me. I can't be without you. I don't deserve you, but I'm begging anyway. Please love me, and let me love you. If you do, I promise you will never regret granting me that grace."

She remained quiet for a second, trying to slow her racing heart so she could have a clear thought. This wasn't something she could rush into. Then she looked up into those electric eyes of his, and the noise was silenced in her head. This man was her home, her refuge. Now it was time for her to be those things to him.

"I've got two conditions."

"Name them." His words left no doubt he was eager to accept any terms she put forth to make them a reality again.

"You're so lucky I'm a good woman. Otherwise, I could take you for everything you're worth."

"And I'd gladly give it."

She didn't doubt it.

"First, we never keep things from each other

again. Aléx, we've been so locked in our own heads, carrying around old hurts and pains and not being there for one another, and it almost ruined us. We only deal in truth from now on."

"Agreed."

Satisfied with his answer, she continued. "The second is, you've got to give me one of your incredible foot massages at least once a week after the baby is born. There is no way I can exist without them."

His laughter shook them, and before she knew it, she was joining him. The heavy tension they'd dragged around unnecessarily was laid by the wayside. They'd made it through the storm, and instead of tears, there were smiles and laughter.

"Your conditions are agreeable, Treasure. Shall we kiss to seal this accord?"

The baby chose that moment to kick, and because of the position they were lying in, Aléx felt the strength of it against his own torso. He placed his hand on her belly where he'd felt the kick and soothingly rubbed it until the little one calmed down.

"Dearest One. You mustn't kick your mother that way when I'm trying to secure our future. It's rude."

"That's rich coming from a man who told me I owed him a baby."

He didn't deny it. From the smug look on his

face, he didn't even have the decency to feel ashamed. Instead, he placed a kiss on her forehead before staring down into her eyes.

"I'm better now, thanks to you. Let me repay that favor ten thousandfold every day for the rest of our lives."

The amusement left his face, and she could see the intensity of his feelings in his eyes and the straight set of his jaw. She kissed him back, placing a hungry kiss on his mouth and moaning when he matched her press for press and stroke for stroke.

This new Aléx, the one who wore his feelings on his face, he was the man she wanted by her side. They'd gone through hell for him to emerge, but he was here, alive, and she was in his arms.

He broke away, leaving them both panting with chests heaving.

"Does that mean yes?" His words were thick with love, passion and need. He needed her to say yes.

"That means yes, ten thousandfold for the rest of our lives."

EPILOGUE

"Look at Auntie's baby!"

Aléx watched as his sister-in-law fell in love with his daughter. He couldn't blame her. His Dearest One had been sublime perfection since she'd made her entrance into the world a few hours ago.

Aléx looked down at his wife in her hospital bed. He was in awe. She was the real hero of the day, laboring for hours and then bringing their daughter safely into the world. He laced her fingers in his and brought them to his lips, whispering "I love you" against them.

"All right, you two." Reigna's warning tone pulled their attention away from each other and onto her. "Y'all had better keep all that kissing to a minimum or you're going to be right back in here in nine to eleven months."

"You're a whole lie." Regina deadpanned. "Now that I know what contractions feel like, I'm gonna need a few years to recover before we even contemplate trying that again."

Before the two sisters dissolved into a fit of giggles, Aléx walked over to Reigna with his hands out and waited for her to place his sleeping daughter in his hands. Once he had her securely in his arms, the baby cooed as if she knew this would be one of two safest places for her from now until eternity.

Looking at his daughter, Aléx couldn't believe how far the four adults in the room had come in less than a year. Regina's hair care line was primed for a successful launch in six months. The fear she'd had that her sister wouldn't understand disappeared when Reigna, outside of Aléx himself, had become Regina's biggest supporter. Her support had healed whatever hurt their past shared trauma had created, making the sisters closer than anyone could've imagined, even for twins.

He and Jasiri had mended their rift. Letting down his guard had meant Aléx had a trusted confidant to help him through his low spaces. It also meant he got to experience Jasiri's joy and exuberance for life firsthand. Aléx hadn't understood how much he'd missed experiencing Jasiri's bold and carefree personality until he'd let the man in again. Now that he'd found the strength to, he and Jasiri were closer than two brothers could ever be. He trusted that man with everything, including the precious little girl sleeping in his arms.

Aléx stood in front of Jasiri and handed him the newborn.

"King Jasiri, would you honor my daughter by giving her your blessing?"

Jasiri beamed with pride in much the same way he had when Aléx had blessed Jasiri's daughter four months ago.

"It would be my honor."

He motioned for Aléx to remove the Nyeusian standard from his nearby satchel. Draping it over the baby, he looked at Aléx and said, "Have the two of you decided on a name yet?"

Aléx nodded, his heart pinching inside his chest with bittersweet love.

"It is an Obsidian tradition that the heir bears the names of the kings or queens who came before."

Aléx glanced over at his wife, and she proudly said, "We decided to name her after two of the greatest queens in the Obsidian royal line. Nairobi Carisse."

"Regina," Aléx finished. "If we're going to name her after the greatest Obsidian queens, then her mother's name must be included too."

Regina was shocked. Aléx hadn't discussed it with her because he knew she'd say no. In his eyes, there was no contest. She was the greatest queen Obsidian Island had ever seen. She'd given him back his life, loved him, and made him a father. To him, there were no greater feats accomplished in his royal bloodline.

Jasiri nodded, arranging the standard gently around the precious babe.

"Princess Nairobi Carisse Regina, daughter of Queen Regina, issue of the great King Aléxandros, standard bearer of the Obsidian royal line of succession, heir apparent, and crown princess of the Obsidian throne."

He slowly swiped a reverent thumb across the child's head before he spoke again.

"May you possess the wisdom of all your ancestors so that you will rule with forethought and foresight."

He flattened his hand on the babe's chest, and Aléx's shoulders sat a bit straighter and his chest a bit broader as he watched Jasiri continue with the ceremony.

"May your heart be filled with compassion and kindness, so that you will rule with grace and benevolence."

Jasiri lifted the open hand the princess had strewn across half her face.

"May your hands be as open and strong as your heart so that you may carry and comfort your people and your nation through the sorrows life will inevitably bring."

Nairobi gave a long stretch before she settled against Jasiri's chest again. Jasiri gently clasped her foot between his forefinger and thumb, and the princess was rewarded with an enamored smile on the neighbor king's face.

"May your feet be strong and sturdy, so that you may stand as a beacon to your people in times of light and darkness."

Aléx watched Jasiri make eye contact with him, and he could've sworn he saw a hint of glass in the Nyeusian king's eyes. Could the big strong king be fighting back tears? He wouldn't have been the first man in the room today. Aléx had cried multiple times since the doctor had laid the new baby in his arms. And he didn't feel the least bit bad about it.

"To Princess Nairobi of the Obsidian royal line of succession, may your reign be long and may your legacy live on forever."

This time it was Aléx who motioned to the sisters, and they each joined Aléx in repeating after Jasiri in unison.

"May your reign be long, and may your legacy live on forever."

Aléx leaned down to his wife, placing a wisp of a kiss across her puffy lips. Joy filled him as he sat down on the edge of the bed and whispered in her ear, "May our love reign long, and may its legacy live on forever."

She returned his peck, her eyes slightly exhausted, no doubt from all the work she'd put in today. The strength of this woman never ceased to amaze him.

As she'd said, she'd had enough love to carry them to this place where elation washed away the darkness in his heart and left it full of light and possibility. She shouldn't have had to bear that alone, and he would make certain her reward would be a husband who would love her through joy and tribulation. He would love her to life and through life until he breathed his last breath, and then from the grave, he would continue to love her into eternity.

She placed a hand over Aléx's heart, and it beat stronger for her. She looked up into his eyes before she repeated, "May our love reign long, and may its legacy live on forever."

* * * * *

If The King's Pregnancy Proposition
*left you wanting more, then don't miss
the previous installment in
the Crowning a Devereaux duet,*
Royal Bride Demand*!*

*Or why not try the other installments in
the Devereaux, Inc., miniseries,
published by Harlequin Desire?*

A Very Intimate Takeover
Backstage Benefits
One Night Expectations
Secret Heir for Christmas

Available now!

Get up to 4 Free Books!

We'll send you 2 free books from each series you try PLUS a free Mystery Gift.

Both the **Harlequin Presents** and **Harlequin Medical Romance** series feature exciting stories of passion and drama.

YES! Please send me 2 FREE novels from Harlequin Presents or Harlequin Medical Romance and my FREE gift (gift is worth about $10 retail). After receiving them, if I don't wish to receive any more books, I can return the shipping statement marked "cancel." If I don't cancel, I will receive 6 brand-new larger-print novels every month and be billed just $7.19 each in the U.S. or $7.99 each in Canada, or 4 brand-new Harlequin Medical Romance Larger-Print books every month and be billed just $7.19 each in the U.S. or $7.99 each in Canada, a savings of 20% off the cover price. It's quite a bargain! Shipping and handling is just 50¢ per book in the U.S. and $1.25 per book in Canada.* I understand that accepting the 2 free books and gift places me under no obligation to buy anything. I can always return a shipment and cancel at any time. The free books and gift are mine to keep no matter what I decide.

Choose one: ☐ **Harlequin Presents Larger-Print** (176/376 BPA G36Y) ☐ **Harlequin Medical Romance** (171/371 BPA G36Y) ☐ **Or Try Both!** (176/376 & 171/371 BPA G36Z)

Name (please print)

Address _____ Apt. #

City _____ State/Province _____ Zip/Postal Code

Email: Please check this box ☐ if you would like to receive newsletters and promotional emails from Harlequin Enterprises ULC and its affiliates. You can unsubscribe anytime.

Mail to the Harlequin Reader Service:
IN U.S.A.: P.O. Box 1341, Buffalo, NY 14240-8531
IN CANADA: P.O. Box 603, Fort Erie, Ontario L2A 5X3

Want to explore our other series or interested in ebooks? Visit www.ReaderService.com or call 1-800-873-8635.

---

*Terms and prices subject to change without notice. Prices do not include sales taxes, which will be charged (if applicable) based on your state or country of residence. Canadian residents will be charged applicable taxes. Offer not valid in Quebec. This offer is limited to one order per household. Books received may not be as shown. Not valid for current subscribers to the Harlequin Presents or Harlequin Medical Romance series. All orders subject to approval. Credit or debit balances in a customer's account(s) may be offset by any other outstanding balance owed by or to the customer. Please allow 4 to 6 weeks for delivery. Offer available while quantities last.

Your Privacy—Your information is being collected by Harlequin Enterprises ULC, operating as Harlequin Reader Service. For a complete summary of the information we collect, how we use this information and to whom it is disclosed, please visit our privacy notice located at https://corporate.harlequin.com/privacy-notice. Notice to California Residents – Under California law, you have specific rights to control and access your data. For more information on these rights and how to exercise them, visit https://corporate.harlequin.com/california-privacy. For additional information for residents of other U.S. states that provide their residents with certain rights with respect to personal data, visit https://corporate.harlequin.com/other-state-residents-privacy-rights/.